Smith's
MONTHLY

Every Month Original
Novels, Stories, and Articles

USA Today Bestselling Writer
Dean Wesley Smith

TABLE OF CONTENTS

SHORT STORIES

FULL NOVEL

NONFICTION

SMITH'S MONTHLY ISSUE #42

Introduction
THE BIRTH OF A SERIES

The book in this volume is the second book in the Mary Jo Assassin series. No worries, it stands alone. You don't have to read *Death Takes a Partner,* the first book in the series, to read this one.

But I never intended Mary Jo Assassin to become a series. Just never crossed my mind when I wrote the first Mary Jo Assassin short story.

And then a second short story.

The idea of a series with Mary Jo had still never crossed my mind when I wrote the first novel. I just thought it would be a standalone book. But I really liked the character and her attitude and it seems others did as well.

So a bunch of time went past after I finished that first novel and I sort of forgot about Mary Jo Assassin. I was working on my Thunder Mountain series or my Seeders Universe series and so on.

But then one fine afternoon, I was talking with Allyson Longueira, the publisher of WMG Publishing, and she brought up Mary Jo and the branding of the covers we had done on that first book. And somehow in that conversation I told her I would look for a piece of art for a second book.

Just for fun.

Still no intent to write a second book.

But playing around on an art sight a few days later, I found the wonderful photo art that is on the cover. It was a full color art photo. You can see it on the cover of this issue of *Smith's Monthly.*

I gave the photo to Allyson and she changed the art and made it into the wonderful black and white book cover with color only on the blue diamond.

Stunning book cover.

And with the cover in place, Mary Jo said to me that it was time to tell the next story.

So I started with a short story I had written and jumped the novel from there

Thanks for the Support

Dean Wesley Smith

with a note on my computer that said, "Bring in a diamond somewhere."

Turns out the entire book rotates around diamonds. Guess if I tell my subconscious I need something, it goes all the way.

So Mary Jo now has a second book and Mary Jo Assassin is now officially a series. Allyson has even done the third cover for a book I haven't even thought about yet. That book is called *Death Takes it Raw*.

Oh, my, looks like I might just be nagged by an assassin to write another book. And I don't mean Allyson. I do mean Mary Jo. There will be a third book and more in this series now.

So thanks, Allyson, for the gentle nudge and the fantastic covers that got my creative voice firing. I had a blast writing this twisted mystery and spending time once again with Mary Jo and the other assassins. I hope you enjoy reading it as well.

And thanks, everyone, for the support of this crazy magazine project. It means a lot to me.

—Dean Wesley Smith
July 29th, 2017

Coming Next Issue in *Smith's Monthly*

DRY CREEK CROSSING

A Thunder Mountain Novel

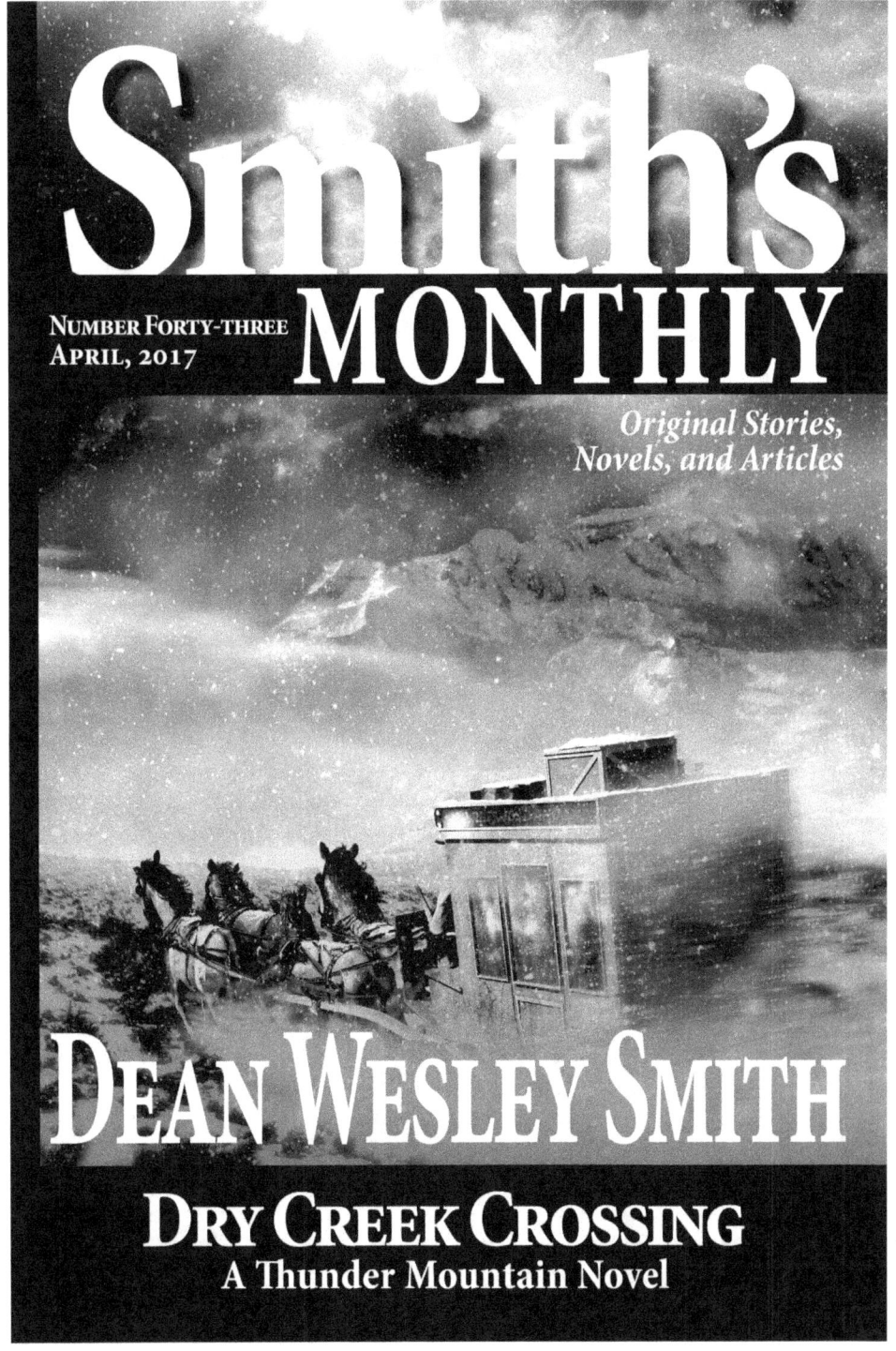

Date Night for ghosts.

Ghost agents and former superheroes need date nights. Marble Grant and her beautiful partner, Sim, hit the bars just as any young and healthy couple, even though they died a while back.

Sex occupies their minds, plus drinking. Maybe too much drinking.

So can two drunk ghosts save the day? With Marble Grant, who knows.

DELIGHTFULLY DIZZY
A Marble Grant Story

WHO KNEW GHOSTS could get drunk?

But I was a ghost and most definitely drunk. Tipsy as someone might say. Sloshed. Feeling no pain.

And Sim, my beautiful blonde, very hot partner, also seemed to be under the influence of the ten or so Gray Goose vodka sliders we had managed to put down. Her wonderful intense blue eyes didn't seem to be able to focus.

I know I was focused on her. I wanted to get us both back to our apartment, get us both out of these slinky dresses we had poured ourselves into earlier, and see what kind of trouble we could get into on our huge soft bed.

At least before one of us got sick and had to hold the other's hair over the toilet. Got a hunch that was coming as well unless we ghosts had a way of suddenly getting sober.

Damn wouldn't that be nice.

We were in our newest favorite bar just off the strip.

Music was loud, the dancing fast, the drinks real, and everyone in the place was young. The lighting moved from a strobe to the beat to dark and moody. Somewhere under all the bodies I figured there was dark wood furniture, a wooden floor, and enough spilled liquor to glue a house together without nails.

At first we had taken turns being inside hot young couples, dancing, enjoying how all they wanted was to get laid. It was infectious, I can say that much. Young hormones were powerful things.

And after we had five or six drinks, we just started dancing on our own, not caring how many people went through us because everyone was thinking the same thing we were thinking about getting laid. We were in love with each other and this was our night out, date night, so we didn't care.

But wow was I horny.

And drunk. Don't forget the drunk part.

About the eighth drink, we found a table and sat. The couple at the table hadn't returned in thirty minutes and from the looks of them on the dance floor, they wouldn't return to do anything but get their things and head for a room. Just watching their young bodies pressing together made me hot.

One thing both Sim and I had discovered early about being ghosts was that the ghost element of everything tasted so much better than the real thing. Food tasted better, sex felt better, and clearly alcohol was more powerful in ghost form as well.

We started on the Gray Goose vodka shooters because two very rich couples at a table in a VIP area were drinking them. We just took the ghost versions of their drinks. The nice thing about being a ghost was the real people never noticed.

But wow did we notice.

Those drinks tasted wonderful and clearly had a kick.

"Is the room spinning?" Sim asked as the sound dimmed slightly. She smiled at me across the table, but her smile was a little sideways.

Oh, oh. We needed to get moving before ghost puke ended up all over everything.

"That's just me wanting to get you home in bed and do wonderful things to that body of yours," I said, standing and offering her my hand, surprised I had managed a full sentence in my drunken state.

"We can't drive," she said. "We're too drunk.

Then she giggled.

Damn I loved her giggle.

I was just about to jump us to our wonderful bed when the couple returned to their table and he went right through me.

Suddenly my delightfully dizzy feeling was gone, replaced by total horror.

This guy was planning on killing his date tonight after they finished. That way his wife would never know he had cheated on her.

He had done the same to some poor girl a year ago at this same real estate conference he was attending.

The guy's name was Radford. He sold real estate back in the Midwest and was here only for the conference. He was cold and calculating and I'll tell you, his mind could kill a girl's buzz faster than dropping a cell phone in a toilet.

I pulled Sim toward me and she went through him as well. I needed my partner on the same page with me on this one. Two drunk ghosts might be equal to one sober one.

I hoped.

Sim shivered and looked at the guy like a mother about to scold a child.

"Now that's not right," she said, staring at the monster. "You can have sex with someone without killing them, you pervert."

I laughed and hugged my partner around the shoulders.

"You take the girl," I said. "Make her so dizzy she's got to sit down and then throw up."

Sim laughed and gave me a drunken thumbs-up. "Now that should be easy and I might just join her. Damn room is spinning like someone jacked up the speed on a merry-go-round."

She went into the woman who instantly sat down where I had been sitting, looking green.

Sim appeared, shaking her beautiful head and frowning. A drunken frown, but still a frown.

"She was planning on killing him tonight so her husband wouldn't find out." Sim stared at both of them. "He's evil and she's an ice queen. What a pair. They deserve each other."

"What the hell?" I asked.

"A real winner," Sim said. "Take a look but don't overstay your welcome. She's about to blow."

I went over and went inside the woman who was clearly about to be sick. Sim was right. Last year she had killed a guy she slept with to make sure her powerful husband back East wouldn't find out what she had done here while on a trip with the girls.

I stepped back out of the ice queen to join Sim just as the woman lost part of her drinks all over her expensive slutty black shoes and his expensive silk suit pants.

"Get him to toss his cookies in her hair," Sim said, laughing.

I jumped inside of the monster and figured out quickly how to make him very dizzy and sick to his stomach and then positioned him in such a way that he was standing over her, like he was trying to help her.

Then I got the hell out before how he was feeling made me sick as well.

He threw up some really disgusting blue and black stuff all over his future victim's hair and down inside the back of her low-cut dress.

Oh, yuck, that had to feel damn awful.

Standing back out of the splatter zone, Sim applauded like watching a kids' soccer game.

The real people at neighboring tables were moving as well, most laughing.

When he did that, she sat bolt upright, a look of pure evil in her eyes, then the look in her eyes blurred and got confused and she retuned fire, spraying his suit jacket and crotch with some really vile red and pink remains of a drink she more than likely regretted drinking.

That caused the evil bastard to jump back and then return fire as well, hitting the front of her dress and legs this time.

She tried to stand in disgust, slipped on the slime-covered surface and went down into the mess.

He then threw up on her again.

Now over the years I had enjoyed myself a lot in bars, but never had I laughed this hard before.

Sim was bent over double, laughing as well.

And all the live people had formed a circle around the couple, out of splatter range of course, and were laughing.

And holding their noses.

The smell was something awful.

Both of the evil humans were dripping vomit. Their planned night of sex and murder was finished, of that I had no doubt.

He managed to take a deep breath of the foul-smelling air and not throw up again.

Then, with a shudder, he turned and with the crowd opening a path for him, headed for the front door, leaving his future victim on the floor crying.

If she wasn't such a cold-blooded killer, I would have felt bad for her.

Not a chance.

"Remember their hotel and room numbers?" I asked Sim, who grinned once again when the woman lost even more of the pink drink on a poor bouncer's shoes.

"I sure do," she said. "You thinking we deal with them early in the morning?"

"I am," I said.

She reached out and took my hand, giving me that seductive smile I loved so much. "Take me home and do rude things to me."

I took us to our bathroom in our wonderful condo and then standing under a wonderful warm shower, we undressed each other, peeling slowly out of our dresses.

And I don't think that anything we did to each other was rude.

Nope.

However, what we did to the two killers the next morning was rude by any measure, ending with the police hauling both of their hung-over asses to jail for their crimes from the previous year. For some reason they both felt they had to confess over and over.

But that night, after we got home from the bar, still feeling the drinks, every wonderfully dizzy moment with the love of my ghost life was magnificent. I would talk about it, but a good girl doesn't have sex with another good girl and tell.

That wouldn't be proper.

And trust me we were both damn good.

But I do have to admit, what Sim did with her tongue for about thirty minutes was far from proper. Not rude, but not proper either.

I'm dead and I called it heavenly.

More Marble Grant Stories
Available at your favorite booksellers.

The First Ghost of a Chance Novel
*Available in electronic format or print
at your favorite booksellers.*

USA *Today* Bestselling Writer

DEAN WESLEY SMITH

THE FIVE ROADS
TAVERN AND EATERY
A Five Roads Story

The Five Roads Tavern and Eatery exists only for those who need it.

Magic exists in The Five Roads, a bar where a person makes a choice as to which road to walk.

The bar sits firmly on that junction of choice for many people.

Now, on a beautiful New York morning, Ellin understands a little more about the better road she travels.

THE FIVE ROADS TAVERN AND EATERY

AROUND ME, THE Manhattan traffic was the constant dull roar and honking of horns that I was used to. I flat loved this city. The July day would be warm, but in the shadows of the trees and buildings along Lexington Avenue, the early morning air remained cool, almost to the point I wish I had pulled on a jacket over my blue cotton blouse before leaving my apartment.

It wouldn't matter. The Five Roads always held a perfect temperature in the heat of summer or dead of winter. Magic can do that for you, if you know how to use it. Whoever had built The Five Roads knew how to use magic in so many ways, of that there was no doubt.

I was only just starting to learn about much of it.

I had never met the mysterious owner and builder of The Five Roads. From what I understood from long-time patrons, the bar had just been there to be found by those who needed it since the beginning of the city.

A normal person walking down Lex would never see the four steps down and the huge, carved wooden door that led into The Five Roads.

And they would never see the sign over the door. The first time I had seen it, I had needed to see it.

That's the way The Five Roads worked.

I was in the process of divorcing from an abusive bastard and just looking for a place to go and sit and be safe from him and his friends who seemed to take great delight in making my very existence torture.

That morning my soon-to-be ex had decided I needed a lesson in how to stay and he beat me so bad I needed a hospital.

I had run and found the door to The Five Roads. I thought he was chasing me and the bar seemed perfect, safe, and welcoming, so I went in.

A month later I was tending bar and no longer bothered by my ex since some of the customers in The Five Roads took a liking to me and made sure my dear old abusive ex-husband would never bother another woman. The last time I saw him, he was shriveled up and delusional in a long-term state-care facility.

I stood on the sidewalk for a moment to let myself enjoy the wonderful New York morning, then turned and went down the steps to The Five Roads.

The big wooden door was unlocked, at least to me, and I pushed it open and went into the dim interior, welcoming the smell of wood polish and fresh fruit.

The lights over the bar were turned on to normal and Blish, the bar manager I reported to, was there cutting oranges for drinks. He clearly had already polished a lot of the wood in the place, and that was no small chore. The inside of the bar was mostly wood.

Polished wooden tables, large wooden chairs, wooden floor, and tall tree-like wooden pillars. Normally I would have thought that too much wood, but it made the place feel like it was outside in a forest instead of down four steps off a crowded sidewalk in New York.

I had a hunch that was also part of the magic in the place. I didn't have any magic, but I sure didn't question it either. I guess that made me the perfect bartender.

That and everyone said my smile and green eyes could light up a room and I could tell a dirty joke with the best of them.

"Mornin' Ellin," Blish said without looking up as the door closed behind me.

Blish was tall and wide in the shoulders, as if he worked out all the time. His hair was almost white even though he was clearly young. I knew nothing at all about his private life. All I knew about him was that he opened every morning and then left when The Five Roads was ready to open for business.

"It is a wonderful morning out there," I said as I headed toward the bar. It was also a polished oak wood and filled the back wall directly across from the main door. The mirrors behind the shelves on the back-bar made the entire room look far larger than it actually was. Luckily I was thin and had a good ass because those mirrors allowed the customers to sit at one of the twelve bar stools and stare in the mirror at my ass.

I honestly didn't mind at all. Flirting was something else I did easily and for fun, both with men and women. Though not once since I had started here had I been tempted to leave with anyone.

And I planned on keeping that streak alive for some years to come. I was doing just fine on my own, thank you very much.

I went into the back room and dropped my small purse and made sure my long brown hair was combed and pulled back, then went back to help with what was left of the morning set-up.

It was at that moment that the big front door opened and a woman walked in.

Now this woman looked so bad that I doubted even the magic of The Five Roads could help her. She only had on one tennis shoe and her expensive silk blouse was ripped off her right shoulder. She had on a form of designer jeans that now looked like someone had dragged them through oil.

She had short brown hair and a large bruise under her right eye that looked like it was going to swell her eye shut very shortly.

She stopped, clearly confused as both Blish and I headed toward her.

She saw Blish and started to turn.

"I got this," I said to Blish and he instantly stopped and backed away to the bar.

I got to her just in time to get her to a chair before she slumped to the floor. She was a mess. Someone had really beaten her badly and I had no doubt she needed medical help.

I knew the feeling. My ex had done the same to me a number of times until I had had the courage to finally run.

"Get the medical kit," I said to Blish and he nodded and turned toward the back room.

"I'm Ellin," I said softly to the woman, kneeling down in front of her. "You are in a safe place now."

She had deep brown eyes and for a moment those eyes focused on me and she nodded before she vanished back into the horrors in her own mind.

I knew those horrors well. I still visited them regularly in my dreams and with my counselor.

Blish put the medical kit on the bar and didn't come around. I left the woman just long enough to get the kit and get back to her.

"Can I clean up some of your cuts?" I asked, noticing that blood was slowly staining her blouse from cuts on her arms and the dark marks on her jeans was more than likely blood as well.

She nodded and I got out some antiseptic and pads and carefully worked on one of the lighter cuts on the back of one of her hands. I wasn't a doctor and this woman I was sure was going to need one. But right now I was dealing more with her fear. If I did something slightly wrong, she would bolt.

I know in her position, I would have.

She had to feel this place was safe.

I worked on one small cut for a moment, then turned back to Blish. "Can you get Connie to come in?"

He nodded, knowing not to speak. He took out his phone and stepped into the back room.

"Connie is a regular here and a medic," I said to the woman. "She helped me when my ex beat me like this."

Again the woman came alive in her eyes and looked at me, then said softly, "Thank you."

I noticed that her mouth was also bloody as she spoke. Clearly she had lost a few teeth in whatever had happened. I just hoped Connie's magic was strong enough for this one. I doubted this woman could handle a hospital at this point, even though that was where she needed to be.

Hospitals were not a safe place when a predator was stalking you, no matter how much the hospital tried to be.

Blish came out of the back room and gave me a thumbs-up as I started to work gently on another deep cut.

The woman just sat still, clearly in deep shock.

A moment later Connie appeared out of the back room and came around the bar. The patrons of this bar with real magic could come in and out when they wanted and clearly Blish had told Connie to come through the back room, even though there was no door back there leading outside.

Connie came around and pulled up a chair and sat facing the woman, nodding to me that I should just ease back a little. I did.

"My name is Connie. Would it be all right if I helped you some with your physical wounds?"

Connie's voice was soft and firm and there wasn't a threatening thing about her. Connie was in her mid-thirties, with silver hair and a smile that felt like it could warm up a room. She had dark brown eyes that seemed to see everything around her.

The woman nodded and then said, "Yes, thank you."

Connie glanced at me. "Would you get us a glass of water and do you have a fresh blouse you might lend this woman in the back room?"

"I do," I said.

I stood and turned for the bar. When I glanced back there was a warm, shimmering orange glow surrounding the woman. She had her eyes closed and as I watched, the cuts on her hands healed and the swelling started going down on the side of her face.

I know Connie had done that for me as well my first time here. All I remembered about it was the warmth and the feeling of being cared for.

I had three extra blouses hanging in the back for when I spilled something on myself. As I went by Blish he whispered, "I'm headed out. Better I get out of here for this. Good job."

I nodded and when I came back out with the blouse he was gone.

An orange glow still surrounded the woman. But now, except for the torn blouse and the missing shoe, she was looking almost well.

I really, really loved the magic of this wonderful place.

The glow faded and was gone as I reached the two of them.

I handed the glass of water to Connie who offered it to the woman. She nodded thank you and then drank a little, clearly surprised her mouth was also healed.

"I have no idea what you did, but I am very grateful," the woman said.

"We do what we can," Connie said. "The rest will be up to you."

I handed the woman the white cotton blouse and she nodded thank you and took off her ripped silk blouse and slipped it on. Her bra cost more than I made in a month and she was clearly far, far too thin.

Connie waited for the woman to button up the blouse, then leaned forward. "Can you tell us who did this to you?"

The woman seemed lost again in her eyes, then came back and said clearly, "My husband."

"Do you have a place to go to get away from him?" Connie asked.

I remember that same question my first time here.

"Not in the city. He is very rich. I'm afraid there is nowhere to go."

For a moment I thought she might cry, but she pulled it together, sat up straight and looked at Connie.

I was impressed. This woman was strong. Strong enough that The Five Roads had let her in the door.

"Do you have a place outside of the city?" Connie asked.

"My parents live in Chicago. I could go there. But I have no money and he would know to look for me there. He considers me his property."

She was right. I knew the bastard type. My ex was the same way. It hadn't started out that way when we met. It never did.

"Money is not an issue," Connie said. "And he will never follow you or bother you again, I can promise you that."

The woman looked confused. "How can you make that promise?"

"The same way you could be healed of all those terrible wounds," Connie said simply.

The woman started to open her mouth, then instead looked down at her hands that just a little bit before had been cut and bloody.

After a moment the woman shut her mouth and nodded.

"You would do that for me?"

"The Five Roads found you and allowed you in," Connie said. "That is only a part of what we do here."

I knew that also as a fact.

"Each of us has five major roads we can travel in our lives," Connie said to the woman. "You made a wrong decision and ended up on one of the bad roads, a road that would have quickly ended up with your death."

The woman nodded to that and said nothing.

I knew for a fact that I would be dead if I hadn't been lucky enough to end up in The Five Roads.

"This place is a gathering place at the junction of the five roads," Connie said. "You can decide to leave here and continue on the same road or pick another road to walk forward on. From here the choice is yours."

The woman nodded. "He had hit me before, but I forgave him. Then I came to

hate him and I suppose he sensed that and this morning he did this to me. I do not know how I escaped. Or how I got here."

Connie nodded.

I remembered that pattern clearly as well.

"I would like to walk a new road, to start my life over."

Connie nodded, but said nothing

"I will do just that even if you decide to not help me," the woman said, her voice firm. "My parents have some resources. I can fight him. I will fight for my freedom. No one will ever hit me or think they own me again."

Connie nodded and again said nothing.

"I want to thank you for whatever you did giving me back my health," the woman said, slowly standing.

She kicked off her one tennis shoe and made no motion to pick it up.

"If I could borrow a phone, I could call a friend to pick me up and get me to the train station. If I can get to my parent's home, I will stand a chance in the coming fight."

Connie smiled with that and stood to face the woman.

"That is all we needed to hear. A friend of this place will be here in one minute to pick you up, get you to the train station, and buy your ticket. She will even have shoes that fit you."

The woman started to say something and Connie held up her hand.

"This fight to recover from what has happened has just begun on your new road. Your husband will never bother you again, that I can promise. But he is only part of the fight you must face. You must heal yourself and discover why you picked that road over other possible roads in the first place."

The woman nodded. "That I understand."

At that moment the front door opened and Whitney walked in. She was a regular and often drank and played darts with two of her best friends from college in the back corner. Whitney was about Connie's age with brown hair longer than mine.

Whitney handed the woman a pair of tennis shoes.

"Thank you," the woman said, sat down and put them on. "They fit perfectly."

"They should," Whitney said, smiling. "They are yours from your closet."

The woman stood, looking stunned.

Whitney then handed the woman a small blue carry purse. "Your driver's license is in there along with a couple of your credit cards and about seven hundred in cash."

"How did you get this? He was there when I left? And you don't even know my name or where I lived?"

Whitney just shrugged.

Now Available
from all your favorite booksellers
in trade paper and electronic editions.

I knew enough about this place to know that nothing really was hidden from the fine folks at The Five Roads.

"It seems your husband got mugged this morning and was sent to the hospital," Connie said, smiling. "I had to put all your injuries somewhere."

The woman looked shocked.

"And don't be surprised if he has a little brain trauma, as you had, from the mugging," Connie said. "He won't be returning to the world in his old form at all."

Silence filled The Five Roads, something I was not used to have happen in this wonderful place. It was as if the entire bar was holding its breath.

Finally the woman smiled and laughed. "I have no idea how you did any of this, healed me like this, but if that bastard ended up beating up himself, I sure won't mind in the slightest."

The deep silence vanished from The Five Roads and everything came back to normal.

"Let's get you to station," Whitney said.

The woman turned to look first at me, then at Connie. "Thank you. Both of you."

"Just stay on your new road and finish the healing process," Connie said.

"I will do just that."

A moment later Whitney and the woman went out the front door and into the warm morning air.

"Will we see her again back here?" I asked, looking at Connie as the big door closed.

Connie shrugged. "I doubt it. I have a hunch that woman won't need to come back here again."

Then Connie turned and looked at me. "Well done with her. You are coming into your magic wonderfully."

"My magic?" I asked, feeling totally stunned. "What magic?"

Connie laughed. "Just keep being who you are and you will understand soon enough. See you later tonight. Girls night out, you know."

And with that she vanished.

I went over and picked up the woman's shoe and ripped silk blouse, put the chairs back where they belonged, and went back to the bar to finish getting ready for the day.

I had been on the wrong road in my life, but with the help of a few wonderful people and this wonderful place, I had decided to walk a new road.

And I was excited about where this new road might take me. Seems from what Connie said, I was only starting down the new road.

As was the woman who had just left.

~

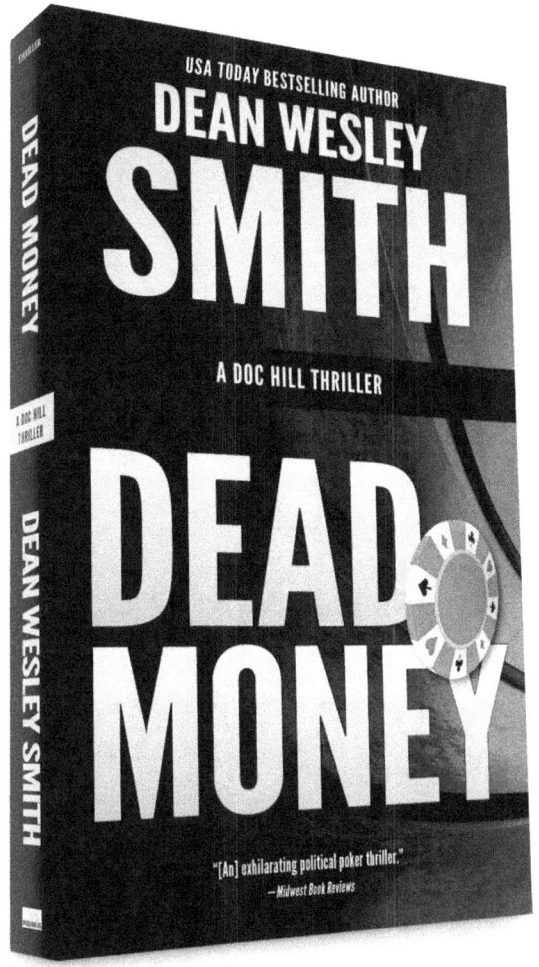

USA TODAY BESTSELLING AUTHOR
DEAN WESLEY SMITH

The
Magic
Bakery

COPYRIGHT IN THE MODERN
WORLD OF FICTION PUBLISHING

A WMG WRITER'S GUIDE

USA Today *bestselling writer Dean Wesley Smith helps writers understand the very nature of their business, how to sell more, and make more money from every story.*

Using the metaphor of a magic bakery, copyright becomes easy to understand, and the writing business makes far more sense.

This book functions as a guide to help writers gain more from every story they write, protect their property, and understand how to expand their business into the future.

Clear, easy to read, and full of insights from a forty-year career writer who understands how every story contains magic. Want more sales, more money from your writing? Come on in to The Magic Bakery.

THE MAGIC BAKERY
A WMG Writer's Guide

Part 2 of 2

Introduction

INDIE WRITERS MAKE great money these days with their small and medium-sized businesses. Some make millions, while at the same time others sell few books.

The writers selling few copies tend to look for reasons why they are not selling. I could spend a lot of time listing all the reasons writers find for a book not selling, but almost always the reason is a very simple business reason.

Inventory.

And a complete failure to understand what they are selling.

But that seemingly simple answer has a vast universe of issues around it. And understanding inventory in publishing takes an understanding of copyright.

So for this book, I am going to extend the metaphor of a Magic Bakery far past its breaking point. Over the years, as I have used this metaphor to help people understand how the business of publishing works, the metaphor seems to help.

And it helps writers understand copyright, the very thing that generates the sales and the money for the business.

So here goes.

Let's open the door to the Magic Bakery, let the wonderful smells of baking bread and fresh doughnuts flow around us. Ignore the racks of cookies sitting in one case and the counter full of wonderful cakes with chocolate frostings.

Head right for the vast cases in the center of the bakery full of pies of all types. All cut and ready to be served either whole or by the slice.

Welcome to your writing business.

The Back Room

Back behind the main counter, beyond that swinging door, is where the magic really occurs.

Flower and flavoring and fresh fruit. Then add sugar and other ingredients and it all comes together in a certain way to create a pie.

A magic pie.

Skill is involved to make the pie, to have it look right, smell right, and most importantly, taste right to the customer.

Years of practiced skill.

Yup, I'm talking about your creation of story. Novel or short story, doesn't matter.

Just like a pie, you take things from the world and combine them in your own unique way to create a wonderful product, a story, for your customers.

Some stories are similar to one another as in a series. Others are as different as a chocolate cream pie would be to a Dutch apple pie. But the customers don't much care.

Sure, each customer has a favorite. Some like the chocolate cream, others go for cherry. But if you have a regular, a true fan, they will try most everything eventually.

A Few Things This Book Will Cover

So in this book, as each chapter goes on, I will talk about opening your bakery when you are still learning how to bake. (Yes, you should, to answer that basic question right off.)

You are learning how to make your pies look like a pie and have a unique taste that customers will return for over and over. That takes time and work. Learning any skill does.

Also, this book will deal some with how the presentation to the customers in your bakery is critical as well.

And how to even get your customers to the front door of your bakery and then what do you do when they walk through the door to help the customer stay, buy, and return later.

All critical aspects to any business.

Real bakeries or magic. Hardware stores or bookstores.

All businesses worry about those exact problems.

But mostly this book will talk about the magic in the pie itself.

You see, just one element of your magic pie is that when you remove a piece, if you do it correctly, that piece can make you money with a customer and yet the pie will remain whole.

The piece of pie that just made you money magically is back in the pie and ready to sell again.

A magic pie.

And that is only one small aspect of the magic.

So stay with me for some chapters here as I extend this metaphor to the extreme in order to help you understand the value, the importance, and the magic of copyright in your writing.

And also help you understand some real reasons why your work isn't selling many copies in this new, crowded world.

You might not like the reasons. But at least you will know how to fix the problems.

And by the end of this book you will know how to have a bakery where lines of customers form out the door to buy your wonderful work.

That is what this book is all about.

Onward.

CHAPTER 1

DIGGING DOWN INTO all the vast areas of how writers sell books and the business of selling fiction, I figured the best way to start this would be on the surface, explaining some real logical, but forgotten (by writers), business concepts.

So an example: A young writer (not in age, but in experience) writes and finishes a first novel. And somehow manages to avoid all the traps of rewriting and letting a peer workshop kill the book. Fantastic!

This is a real event and once published should be celebrated. First novels are important to every writer. Get copies out to family, tell friends where the book can be bought, and then go back to writing the next book.

But sadly, the book sells almost no copies. A few to family and friends and nothing else. No one is reading it. And this is the problem of the new world of indie publishing.

Discouragement for no logical reason. You wrote a book your first readers like, why isn't it selling? And pretty soon the young writer is so discouraged they quit.

Now there are lots of reasons that first novel might not be selling, actually. But the main one concerns the Magic Bakery. And basic business.

SOME HISTORY FIRST

In the old days of traditional publishing only, over ten years ago now as I write this, there was only one path into publishing a book and getting it to readers to buy.

The path was simple: You somehow, through some form, got the book to an editor. This took time and often lots of rejections. Years and years of time.

So the advice back then was to mail the book to someone (editor, agent, subway rat who knew someone who could buy the book for a publisher) and then go back to writing the next book.

This process often took so long and was filled with so many rejections, a writer either quit (most) or kept writing and got better. My first sold novel was my third written novel. And my fourth written novel never saw the light of day.

The time it took allowed writers with drive to improve skills and keep writing. The system forced it.

NOW THE NEW WORLD

There is no system. No one forces a writer to wait to get a book out to readers and no writer should wait. That old system of gatekeepers was too stupid for words.

But now the young writer puts the book out there and there are no sales.

What could be wrong? Why doesn't the book sell?

Clearing out some basic reasons first...

... Your cover sucks and looks like a beginner did it or the art.

... Your sales blurb is so long, so full of plot, and so passive it puts readers to sleep.

... Your opening is so thin, so full of action with no depth, no one would buy it.

... You don't know genre and put the book on the wrong shelf in the electronic stores.

But sure, you might have those things wrong, you fix them, and your book still won't sell.

Why not?

The Magic Bakery is why not.

A PERSONAL STORY FIRST

In early 1977 I decided I wanted to start a used bookstore while I was going to college for a degree in architecture. And not an antiquarian bookstore, but a type of bookstore I had seen starting up in California when I was a golf professional. Basically a paperback exchange.

This was a fairly new concept in 1977 and it sounded like fun. But I had one major issue. I had maybe 400 books I wanted to part with in my collection. So the idea was sort of just a pipe dream until one day I was going up the escalator into my bank when I saw a small For Rent sign on a big metal door at the top of five stairs at the top of the escalator.

You turned right to go into the bank, the stairs went up to the left and to this big metal fire door. I went through the big door into a small lobby. An attorney had a large office ahead, a doctor to the left, and down a dark hallway was the For Rent sign.

An office smaller than most kid's bedrooms. $75 per month. I was hooked.

My wife-at-the-time wanted nothing to do with the idea of starting a business. She was working on her masters. So I promised her I would keep the spending under $200 to start it. I rented the place for $100 for a month counting the deposit, bought about $50 in old pine lumber and built shelves to fill the place. Every wall and in the middle of the small room as well. I bought a used desk for $10 and then took up my 400 books. They looked really, really sad.

Almost the entire store was empty. Pathetic didn't begin to describe it.

So I told my wife-at-the-time I needed to go buy some books and headed out that weekend to find books around the Pacific Northwest. I managed to bring home another thousand paperbacks.

I spent more than $200, but not part of our household funds. I had been playing on blackjack teams in Vegas for a number of years before I met my-then-wife and never told her I had money in cutout paperbacks in my book collections that I had been using to pay for college. The rule about my books was that if they were in a bag, no one touched them. No one bothered to ask me how I could get through college without a loan and only worked a few nights tending bar and driving a school bus. Her parents paid for her expenses.

(I finally told her a few years ago. She is still a friend.)

So I took three hundred out of my own "college fund" and bought the books. They still looked very sad in the room full of empty shelves.

I hung out a sign. No one came at first. Nothing to come for.

So I kept searching for more books, garage sales, you name it, and slowly people started to find the little store down the hall. And I had enough books by that point to sell them or trade them something.

Eventually I grew out of that room, took over the big lawyer's office and then a year later moved the store into its own building down on the street. All while finishing my masters in architecture and then starting law school.

Magic Bakery

The young writer has their one finished book. It is up for sale and no one is buying. Covers, blurbs, opening, and self problem fixed.

No one is buying the book.

Why not?

Imagine you are a customer and you see this great sign for a bakery. Makes your mouth water at the idea of getting something.

You go in. The bell on the door jingles and around you are massive empty shelves and display cases.

All empty except for up near the cash register is this one pie.

If you were the customer, what would you do? Be honest...

You would turn around and walk out, of course. No way are you going to buy from a bakery that only has one product sitting there all alone.

There is no magic to this concept. It is just a logical customer reaction.

You have no product yet.

But that can be fixed...

Now if you stay writing, creating, you will slowly fill the shelves and display cases.

And since in the Magic Bakery nothing spoils, eventually the shelves and the cases will be full. And as you do get more product, some people will stay and buy.

I have over 300 different products in my magic bakery. And many of the products are in different forms.

You know the business concept at play: Selection and flavors. Things to bring the customers to the register to buy.

This concept is not so magic. It is just logical business.

So if you are discouraged about your first or third novel not selling what you hoped, just think of that big empty bakery and go back to writing. Given enough time, you will fill it.

Or at least get enough product in the bakery so that people will start buying as they did in my little bookstore.

CHAPTER 2

SO WHAT MAKES this bakery so magic anyway? Copyright, that's what.

As the *Copyright Handbook* says, "Copyright is the legal device that provides the creator of a work of art or literature, or a work that conveys information or idea, the right to control how the work is used."

So what is so magic about that? All countries in the world have copyright protections in one form or another. As of the writing of this chapter, almost all countries in the world have signed onto one copyright convention or another, agreeing to the basic aspects of copyright protections.

In fact, here in the States, copyright protection was written into the Constitution right from the beginning, it is that important.

But what makes it magic? Actually just one phrase in that definition I gave you is the source of the magic.

"… the right to control how the work is used."

SPOILED COPYRIGHT

Spoiled copyright is a concept that is flat hard to imagine now in this modern world of electronic shelves. As I said in the last chapter, that pie you have sitting there in your shop will never spoil.

Copyright never spoils.

And since we are using a pie as a metaphor for copyright, imagine baking a pie and it will taste just as good five years later as it did on the day you baked it.

Or 70 years later. Or 100 years later if you live for another 30 years after the baking.

This idea that copyright never spoils is almost impossible for writers coming out of traditional publishing to wrap minds around. It took me some time I must admit.

Traditional publishing companies (for decades) used the produce model for books. They treated books like fruit. Not kidding.

The publishers would set a time the book would appear. Then the book would appear and within a set time the book would "spoil" in the eyes of the publisher and bookstores and be pulled and returned to the publisher for credit. For all intents and purposes, that book was dead.

Rotten fruit. Very few books survived that fate. Very, very few.

The reality was that the copyright was just fine. It actually hadn't spoiled. Just the publishers thought of it as dead.

And so did the authors.

And even if an author got the rights back from the company, chances are the book never saw the light of day again.

Writers who got books reverted still had the right to control the use of the book, sure, but the belief was that the copyright had spoiled and the book or story was done. Used up. Rotted fruit.

Then along comes this new world and electronic shelves with unlimited space.

And suddenly all those dead and spoiled books took on a new life.

The magic of copyright never spoiling.

A book that only had four weeks on the shelf 20 years ago now had a chance to find a new audience who weren't even born the first time the book appeared.

My first novel came out in 1989. So basically anyone under 35 would not have read that book unless they found it in a used bookstore. Now that first novel is back out and earning me money for the first time in almost 30 years. And finding new readers who might enjoy it.

It is in this new world that the hard fact of a copyright never spoiling actually started to become a reality to many writers.

It also, after about six or seven years, started to dawn on the major publishers as well, which is why they now buy all rights for the entire life of a copyright. They now understand as well that copyright has value over long periods of time and won't spoil. (They haven't figured out what to do with the rights they are keeping, but they have figured out enough to keep them.)

The magic in the copyright-filled pie now rules. But like with any good magic, you have to know how to unleash the spell. I will get to that.

FIRST SALE AND ELECTRONIC LICENSE

Right now, before I go any farther here in chapter two, I had better get everyone on the same page with a few more basics.

Copyright is the protection of the expression. So when you sell a paper copy of the book, you transfer no copyright. Copyright can only be transferred by a written agreement. You are basically selling a block of paper. Nothing more.

That physical book, that pile of paper, exists and the new owner of the book can sell the block of paper itself. But they have no right to take any of the words from the book and use them.

None. They bought the paper, not the words on the paper.

This is called the First Sale Doctrine and it applies mostly only to paper books.

So in Magic Bakery terms, when a customer in the Magic Bakery buys a piece of your pie (paperback piece), the piece remains in the pie even though the customer gets to enjoy the taste of the pie and walk out of the store with a pile of paper. The piece never leaves the pie.

Magic. An ever-replenishing inventory. Wish I would have had that with my bookstore.

Now we have the new electronic books. So you have the slice of your pie called "Electronic Rights" up on Amazon. **Basically what you have done is rented from the big Amazon Mall some space to include your Magic Bakery inside their mall.**

You also have your Magic Bakery in the Kobo Mall, the B&N Mall, and so on.

When a customer comes through your door and wants a piece of pie in electronic form, they can enjoy it, but they have bought nothing. They have licensed the right to read it only.

Nothing more.

They cannot trade or sell that electronic copy. They own nothing and in fact, you never sold them anything, you licensed to the reader the right to read the work.

Nothing more. **First Sales does not apply to electronic copies.**

So either selling paper copies to a reader or licensing electronic copy to a reader, your pie remains whole sitting in your Magic Bakery.

So over a month's time you sell or license 100 pieces of that pie. The pie has not changed or diminished or spoiled in any fashion.

Every store on the planet wishes for magic inventory like that. Only writers and artists and other copyright holders have it.

WHY ONLY A PIECE?

This is now where the real fun and magic starts to happen.

Why didn't I say that a person buying the paper book didn't buy the entire pie?

Because the entire pie is not just paperback rights. Or electronic licensing rights. Or audio rights.

Say you write a novel. The novel is the pie. The copyright is what you license from the pie, the pieces of the pie, basically.

Each area of the pie is a different right. One small slice is paperback rights, one small slice is hardback rights, one small slice is electronic, one small slice is audio, and on and on.

You never sell the entire pie.

Now going to traditional publishers, they want to buy the entire pie and put your magic in their store. And writers are doing that all the time, allowing their magic pie to leave their bakery.

Visualize it this way: Some person from New York publishing in a suit walks into your Magic Bakery and flops some small amount of money on the counter. You say sure and they take your magic pie and turn and leave your store, leaving that spot on the counter forever empty. FOREVER EMPTY. They walk your magic pie down the mall to their massive anchor store and put your pie in their Magic Bakery.

You have now sold inventory to a store that is competing with your store.

And you will never get that pie back.

In real world terms, this is "all rights for the life of the copyright" contracts. If you see that in your contract for anything, RUN!!

In coming chapters will be a ton more about this problem. And a lot more about how you can divide up the pie, make more money from each slice, and never lose control.

And remember, every story you finish, every novel, every article (including this Magic Bakery book I am writing right now here in front of you) is a new pie. Another product to have in my display cases and on my shelves when a customer comes through the door of my Magic Bakery.

And the larger the store you have, the more product you have, the more customers and the more money you make if you keep the floors swept, the glass on the display cases clean, and a smile on your face.

Frighteningly enough, it really does work that way.

CHAPTER 3

HOW DO YOU slice a magic pie? The answer is simply as many ways as you want.

The wonderful thing about copyright is that you can license any part of it. And you can name the part and dictate the terms and define the shape of the part.

I know this is difficult to imagine. And the pie analogy sort of falls apart because pie is a physical thing that can only be sliced in so many ways.

But imagine the pie is solid and you have a saw that can slice off a piece so thin you can barely see the slice under a microscope.

Yup, you can do that with a magic pie. Honest.

A few broad examples…

Say you were approached by a publisher in a small country you had to go to Google to find on the map. The publisher wanted to translate and print your book only in that country's language. And only in hardback with dust jacket. And only five hundred copies. And only for one year.

You figure out where the country is at and say sure. The contract comes and you get your saw and slice off a tiny, tiny thin license. Translation rights into (country's language only) for hardback only for a run of 500 copies only for only a year.

In a year that tiny, tiny slice will reappear back in the magic pie of copyright for that novel and you can sell it again.

Or say you have a novel headed into a game or movie. You have retained all toy rights. So a manufacture of resin busts comes to you and wants to license the right to make busts of your characters in a limited edition run of one thousand copies signed by the artist.

Out comes the saw and you slice off a tiny, tiny thin license for resin character busts for a limited one thousand copies. And you sell the plush license to the characters to another company and the action figures of the characters to another company and so on and so on.

All limited-time licenses because you understand copyright and contracts.

My wife, Kristine Kathryn Rusch, on her blog, did most of a year about publishing contracts and there is now a book

out of those blogs. That is all basic stuff, but you have to know the basics before you can learn how to use the saw to cut tiny, tiny thin pieces.

And you cannot do that if you have allowed the magic pie to leave your control, your Magic Bakery.

Some Horror Stories
From the Magic Bakery

These are about magic pies leaving your bakery.

First off, agents, especially book and Hollywood agents, are not your friends, folks. Avoid at all costs. All horror stories start and end with the word "agent."

I am not kidding.

Here is a real-life Magic Bakery horror story. Agent sold a writer's novel series to Hollywood. The writer was uninformed about how copyright really worked and the agent was either a crook or stupid or didn't realize what he was doing. Take your pick.

The contract the writer signed sold (not licensed) the Hollywood studio rights to the books in the series. What the writer didn't know about what his agent told him to sign was that it also gave away all control of his characters.

And Hollywood didn't want him writing any more of those characters since they controlled them. Writer lost in the court. He signed the contract.

In other words, what the writer did was stand behind the counter of his Magic Bakery and watch the Hollywood agent carry his magic pie out of the door and take it to another store to make money for someone else.

Another real story.

Remember a writer by the name of Clancy? Wrote this novel called *The Hunt for Red October* that became a major bestseller and a movie. It had a character in it called Jack Ryan.

Clancy stood behind his counter and watched the magic pie leave his bakery for $500 total. Someone else sliced up the pie as they wanted and the pie became a bestselling book and then a movie. Eventually Clancy sued for the right to even use Jack Ryan as a character again in another book.

They settled and he had to pay to use his own character.

Why? Because he let the magic pie that was *The Hunt for Red October* leave his store to make someone else money.

I bet I could come up with another 20 of these horror stories just off the top of my head. After 40 years in this business I have heard so many of them it makes me sick.

Staying With the Analogy

You have a recipe for a wonderful magic pie. You go to all the work to create that pie and use special ingredients that make that pie special.

Then not only do you sell the magic pie you created and let it leave your business, you sell the recipe to the pie as well and all the ingredients. And you sell the right to ever make anything similar to it again.

Why would anyone do that?

I ask myself that every day because it happens 100s, if not 1,000s of times every day in Magic Bakeries all over the world.

Writers do not know what they have, do not understand the value of the golden goose that is the story or novel they created.

So they sell their magic pie for all rights for the life of the copyright to a major publisher. Movie rights, toy rights, translation rights, video, audio, electronic, paper, and on and on. All making someone else money.

And even worse, the writers often sign a contract saying they will not go back and make more magic pies without permission from the buyer of the last magic pie.

Might as well shut that Magic Bakery down. It is finished.

Go to any convention and watch the young writers flocking to agents, listen to the discussions about how to break into traditional publishing.

Then as you listen, realize what they are working so hard to do is make sure their magic pie leaves their Magic Bakery.

Summary Statement

Never ever let your entire magic pie out of your control.

License slices only and then for a limited time only.

Nothing more.

And slice the pieces you do license very, very thin. As thin as you can.

And then keep making new magic pies to fill the shelves.

CHAPTER 4

I STARTED OFF Chapter Three with a question and an answer: "How do you slice a magic pie? The answer is simply as many ways as you want."

But first you have to have a magic pie to slice.

You have to have copyright to license. And that is the rub, the place where so many writers flat run into a massive wall. It takes time and a lot of practice and knocking down personal demons to produce new stories and novels regularly.

Anyone can do it for a short time. A year. Maybe two. But then with just a few cases in their Magic Bakery half full and the rest of the bakery still empty, the writer fades away.

The magic pies don't spoil as I talked about earlier, but they sure gather dust. No one comes through the door and no one keeps up the bakery.

When the writer stops caring about their own business, the business dies. It is called quitting and it is the only way to fail in this modern world of publishing.

Now I understand how hard this is. Clearly understand. And this problem of looking at empty shelves almost got me as well.

So a personal story...

As Kris and I moved from traditional publishing to indie publishing, I got the statement from young writers over and over how easy I had it because I already had work.

Well, I knew how to tell stories, sure. And I had sold millions of books and had made my living in publishing since 1988. Sure.

But the indie world made me into a flat beginner. So when some young writer with three or four or five novels said that I had this huge advantage over them, I just nodded and said nothing.

The only real advantage I had was that I was a better storyteller.

You see, the dirty truth was I had no books. Well, I actually had two, one was my first published novel I had the rights back to and one was a thriller I had written and then tossed in a drawer. And I had a ton of short stories.

For almost all of my career, I was a media writer and a ghost writer. I wrote over one hundred novels under pen names or media books and I didn't own a one of them. I had baked the magic pie in someone else's bakery.

So I had nothing but the short stories and I didn't feel I wanted to bring the thriller or the first novel out right off the bat.

I felt I needed to fill my Magic Bakery.

It felt impossible, I must admit.

I would stand in that Magic Bakery and stare at all the empty shelves and wonder how in the world at my age I would ever fill them. In other words, I had to start my writing career completely over in my 60s.

So with two novel pies sitting in the back room and my bakery almost completely empty except for some shelves of short story pies to one side, I started to work in 2011. All of the shelves were cleaned and polished and just waiting for me to fill them.

Waiting for me to get baking.

I did some more short stories to get started and then lost most of a year to a personal friend's death and estate.

By the time I got back to writing, it was almost 2013. And again I did more short stories to try to get going.

Then in the summer of 2013 I decided I really needed to get baking. I was tired of staring at all the empty shelves.

So I started up *Smith's Monthly,* which needed a novel, four short stories, and a serial every month. And I had to write it all. Every word of a monthly seventy thousand word magazine.

I wrote like crazy that summer to get a few novel pies on the shelf and the first issue came out in October 2013. I am a little behind at the moment here in 2017 as I write this, but I expect to be caught up by October 2017 with the 4th full year without missing a month. And then I plan to start into the fifth year.

Imagine in October a wall of my Magic Bakery will be full of forty-eight magic pies with the sign over the wall *Smith's Monthly* pies.

After four years I now have pies of different sorts filling my bakery.

These nonfiction books taken from blog posts.

The short stories have all been published standalone and a slice of each novel was taken and licensed to WMG to publish standalone.

And I combined slices of the short stories to be in collections and so on. Not counting short stories, last year alone I did twenty-six major books. The year before over thirty. This year will again be over thirty.

I went from having a mostly empty bakery to a decent inventory in my Magic Bakery in four years.

Over a hundred major products and hundreds of short stories.

And the customers are coming, even though I have done very little, if any advertising.

Seems people like the taste of a Cold Poker Gang pie or a Seeders Universe pie or a Poker Boy pie.

This Takes Time

There are a number of hot, young (in numbers of books) gurus out there at this moment preaching how to sell more books by this or that advertising device. Some of the advice is pretty good. And WMG is following some of it in moderation.

But almost without fail, these "experts" have an almost empty Magic Bakery. They have gotten very, very good at driving customers into their empty

store, but have forgotten the reason to have the store in the first place.

Think folks. You might, through some advertising hype or another, go into a store you have never visited. We all do. Standard business stuff. But if you walked into the store with only a few things on the shelves, would you make it a point of going back?

Nope.

In our north Pop Culture Collectables store, we have over 20,000 books and 100,000 comics, toys, cars, games, and collectables of all sorts. It fills four large rooms and when someone comes in they are always surprised at how much we have and they always take time to explore all four rooms.

And they often buy something they didn't even know they wanted.

If they came through the door and we had two collectable cars, an old toy, five used paperbacks, and six used comics in the four rooms, think anyone would bother to stay? Or come back?

Nope.

It has taken us over a year now to get the store as full as it is. And we had all the inventory in the warehouse. It took a year to get it all out and priced.

Things take time.

As writers, we must create our own inventory. And that flat takes time.

But it will never happen if you don't start.

And it will never happen if you quit.

How to Even Start?

First—As I suggest in a number of classes, do an inventory of your Magic Bakery.

Everything. Every article that might be combined into a book, every short story, every novel.

Everything that you own copyright on and have created. Even stuff still in the back room you are too afraid to bring out and put on a shelf.

Second—See if there is any way to create new products with that inventory? You know, take a small slice from five short stories and combine it into a collection. Things like that.

Or get your work up on BundleRabbit so people can ask for the bundling slice of your pies. And so on and so on.

Third—Figure out your hours. How much time do you spend writing each week creating new product? What is stopping you from getting some of the work in the back room out to the shelves?

In other words, find your demons. Check Heinlein's Five Rules and be honest about which rule you are falling down on.

Fourth—Make a five-year and ten-year plan. Expect it to take time to fill your shelves of your Magic Bakery.

Early on, make your focus not on getting customers through the door to be disappointed, but on making your Magic Bakery a place where people will want to return over and over when they do find it.

When you start thinking of your writing as a business and a retail store, it really is amazing how clear some basics about writing become.

I knew this four plus years ago when I started filling my shelves. And I do not plan on slowing down because my bakery really is magic. I have as much room as I need to expand when my inventory starts filling the shelves.

And I plan on doing a lot of expanding over the next 10 years.

CHAPTER 5

I GET A lot of questions about pen names and if writers should use pen names in this modern world of publishing.

So let me use the Magic Bakery to explain my answer to that question.

Now understand, the reason for this book about the Magic Bakery is to help writers understand copyright and the magic power of copyright in this world.

But the metaphor of the bakery can help in business logic as well.

And in sales.

And in promotions. For example, understanding the power of free is clearly illustrated in the Magic Bakery and I will get to that in a later chapter.

But for this chapter, I want to focus on Pen Names.

The New World

In the old world, we had to go down the mall and open up brand new stores and try to fill them every time we started a new pen name.

One store for every pen name.

So most of the time the pen name stores just looked empty and the readers, even if they liked something, had little else to buy.

In this new world, you keep all books under one name.

Think about it. When a customer walks into one of our Pop Culture Collectable stores here on the coast, they see toys, antique jewelry, games, comics, books, cookie jars, clocks, cars, and a bunch more.

We have all the sections in different parts of the store.

So you have a Magic Bakery. A customer walks through the door.

To the right, filling a wall, are all the science fiction pies and cakes. Straight ahead are the romance cakes and rolls, to the left, the mystery pies and snacks.

Then off to one side is the young adult section.

And on all the displays in the middle of the floor are all the short story pies, cakes, rolls, and such.

All are clearly marked so there is no confusion, the descriptions on each shelf clear as to the flavors of the pies.

The customer doesn't have to go to five half-empty stores to find all of your work. They found it all in one store, under one name.

Being Clear

There is no reason at all in this new world of reader-controlled publishing to use a pen name. Keep everything under one name and display that name in bright letters on the outside of your store.

Brand your store to that one name so readers can find everything you do.

They may not like the taste of your mystery blood pies, but they love your romance sweet pies.

Let the readers decide. Give them something to shop for.

Sure, with our stories, we could open a comic store, a toy car store, a collectible card store, a clock store, an antique toy store. Sure.

But it was easier to keep it all in one large store and put it all under one name.

Do the same with your writing.

One name, one Magic Bakery.

CHAPTER 6

I GET QUESTIONS all the time about free. Should an author put up their book for free? How about their first book in a series? Does leaving something up for free forever work?

Interestingly enough, The Magic Bakery works perfectly to illustrate the answer to these questions so writers can decide for themselves.

All I'm going to be talking about in this chapter is basic, standard-retail sales practices. I won't tell you one thing new in the world. You can see some of these practices working every day from grocery stores to music stores.

But explaining these practices to authors who do not understand basic sales of retail has been an issue. And thus extreme myths have built up around the use of free in book sales.

And it seems everyone has an opinion, often not based on anything but "It worked for me for a little bit."

So using the Magic Bakery, let me show you some of the simple ways that free can be an effective sales tool for your products.

And some of the really boneheaded ways to use free that will hurt your business.

Copyright in Free

One quick point here in this book focused on mostly understanding copyright. When you give a story or book away for free, you do not lose the copyright protection on that work in any way.

My Basic Rule of Thumb About Free

Nothing ever sits on a bookstore shelf, real-wood shelf or electronic shelf, for free.

It is a very simple rule and when I say that to someone they automatically think I am against free. I am not. I am against using free in a poor business way. I use free all the time to help sales, as does WMG Publishing.

So now to the Magic Bakery to illustrate why this rule works for me and for others.

First, a simple positive way to use free.

A customer comes into your bakery. You have a wall of about 20 pies that are your novels, some are grouped together because they are series pies. All are priced. You may have a reduced price on a few first pies, but all are priced in a reasonable and fair manner.

You have a large counter in the middle of the room of short story pies, smaller and at a lower price than the larger pies on the wall.

You have specials you are running around the cash register.

And there, beside the specials, near the cash register, on top of a glass counter, you have a plate of bite-sized pieces of your latest creation for readers to sample.

The sign under that plate says, "Take one."

You have maybe a dozen pieces on the plate with small plastic forks and when those pieces of pie are gone, you take the plate to the back to wash. The idea is to get customers, for free, sampling your work so they will buy.

This form of use of free is standard in almost every form of store. You see this a lot in grocery stores. And in bakeries.

For authors, we do this as sample chapters in the back of another book.

Or free short stories for a week on a web site. And so on. Lots of ways to give limited, small samples in this modern world.

The key in sales are LIMITED and SHORT TERM.

Keep free short term and limited and **never put it on a bookshelf anywhere**.

Now the wrong way to use free.

A customer walks through your door and you have a wall of 20 pies in glass cases, all the smaller short story pies in a case in the center, and some specials near the cash register.

And there on your wall are three pies that say, "Free."

And a bunch of short stories that are "Free."

The customer can take an entire pie for free or buy one. As a customer, what would you do? Duh. You take the free pie and leave.

(Or you question the value of any of the pies and leave without anything.)

And, because of copyright, the pie is still sitting there after someone takes it for free. Magic Bakery, remember? So more and more people start hearing you are giving away free pies in your Magic Bakery.

And pretty soon your customers start to change. The only people who come through the door are people who only want the free stuff. They would never buy something under any circumstances, but you are giving your pies away for free, so they take one.

Pretty soon there would be lines out the door to get your free pies and you would make nothing. The free takers would crowd out and devalue the pies you are trying to sell.

That is the wrong use of free for any reason you may want to make up to justify it.

Now discounting is another topic. There are ways to discount first books in a series to entice buyers into getting into a series. This is also a common practice in most stores, actually.

A Personal Example

I live in a small town that has a huge discount mall. Now all smart shoppers know that the big chains mark up the prices before lowering them for the discount stores. Makes the "discount" price look better to those looking for deals.

Now I use the mall as a place to walk on rainy days. And at times, I go into stores to look around. The stores have their "discount" racks clear to the back. The discount racks are what is left of the normal merchandise that hasn't sold and they are just trying to clear.

But to get to that actually discounted stuff, I have to walk through their entire store. And every-so-often, that sales trick gets me and I see something I don't mind paying full price for.

That is a standard retail trick of discounting to get a customer in to buy other stuff.

But not one place in any of those stores is there a free item. Why not? Because they are all businesses, that's why not.

Writers need to learn how to act and think like regular business people.

So How to Use Free in Your Bakery?

A one-day give-away of one of your pies. Only for a very limited time and only for a very limited number.

I try not to laugh in writer's faces who tell me they have "sold" 20,000 books and when I ask, they actually gave away that many books.

Free is not a sale.

Free is free. A sale is when you make something from the exchange. So follow basic retail practices. If you are going to give something away for free, do it for a short time and a limited number.

And then make it special.

And again, never put it on a shelf of any bookstore.

Once again, over the years, I have tried not to laugh when writers go on about how to game Amazon's system and get their book there for free. I have laughed many times, but not in the writer's faces, luckily.

You ever wonder why you have to game the smartest business on the planet at the moment to get something on their shelves for free? Oh, let me think— They don't make any money.

Yet they are a business. You are taking up their shelf space with something that makes them no money.

You walk into our Pop Culture Collectable stores here in town and there isn't one thing on the shelves for free. So do we give things away at times? Sure. Free comic book day once a year. Things like that. Promotions that are limited and short term to bring customers into the store to buy other things.

Limited and short term.

There is no reason at all for us to go to the time and energy to get inventory and then put it on our shelves for free. No reason for any business to do that.

And certainly no reason for you to do that in your Magic Bakery.

Just imagine walking into a pie shop and there is a wall of pies that all look great, and five or six of them say, "Free" under it. Try to imagine that.

If you can't imagine that, good. But if you want to start learning how to use free correctly, then start looking around at other businesses outside of electronic books and see what they do with free.

In the business and sales world, free is a powerful, powerful tool if used correctly and for the right reasons.

Make sure your Magic Bakery is a place someone can come to buy your wonderful work. And that free is used in ways (not on the shelves of your bakery) to entice buyers into your bakery.

Free is short time, limited supply, and never on the major bookstore shelves.

Simple Magic Bakery rules-of-thumb that are nothing more than standard retail business practices.

CHAPTER 7

I KNEW I was going to need to talk about this topic in a chapter and honestly, have dreaded it. Writers, especially newer writers have no understanding of the value of their own work and how others value it.

So with that problem in mind, I am going to try to add a level of understanding of value of copyright to this book. For most of you, I will fail at this, but at least I can say I tried right here in Chapter Seven.

I'm calling this chapter "Perceived Value" of the inventory in the Magic Bakery.

I cannot even begin to count the hundreds and hundreds of times I have heard a new writer say, "I'm new so I should give my stuff away or sell it for only 99 cents."

I will not get into a pricing discussion here. There are lots of other places out there in the vast world of the inner-tubes to shout about your price being better or worse than another price. Go to it.

I am talking about "Perceived Value."

The Dollar Store

Here in the US, there are numbers of chains of stores known for selling things at one dollar. To make sure I was correct in my perceived value of the goods in the Dollar Store, I stopped by the one here on the coast a few days ago.

Lots of small toys, all cheap. Lots of household stuff you could get for a buck in any supermarket.

Everything that was either normally a buck in another store or some cheap knockoff. The entire store.

Now, if I had gone in there looking for a fine bottle of wine, I would have been very disappointed. But I went in there knowing I would be finding exactly what I found. Cheap stuff worth less than a buck.

My "Perceived Value" of that store was right on. I went in expecting cheap and I got cheap. Both in price and quality of the goods.

Let me repeat that: **I got cheap price and a cheap quality of the goods.**

And I was not surprised.

So I log onto a website for a writer I do not know. (Most writers, both experienced and new. I have no way of knowing the difference. And neither do readers.) And I see nothing but free and 99 cent books. What do I expect?

More WMG Writers' Guides
from all your favorite booksellers
in trade paper and electronic editions.

I expect a cheap and lower level of goods.

And since I like to be entertained and only have so much reading time, I will go find another author. Yes, I will pay more. But my two hours of reading won't be wasted.

Quality wine vs. a buck bottle of whine. Sorry, I like a good wine.

Readers are no different. (Sure, there are the only buy cheap or free reader and they sometimes find something worth reading. I got that. Not my customer.)

The Discount Mall Principle

Perceived value is a major art form in discount malls. We have a massive discount mall here and all of the stores in that mall show the original price on every item and then the discount price and the sale price and then for today only take off another 25% if you can stand on one leg and snort.

But that original price is right there on the tag. You can get a $200 coat for today only if you snort loud enough for $49.99. The customer has a perceived value of the coat at $200. Wow, what a deal and they grab it.

Also top brand-name stores are in the mall. Nike for example. Just by walking in that door the customer knows of the perceived value of a Nike shoe.

The Magic Bakery Value

Since you own your Magic Bakery and create all the product, you have the freedom to set your own prices. A logical way to do that is to figure out what other books in your genre are selling for. Then look at what Amazon suggests is a sweet spot.

In other words, toss out all your emotions about the lack of value of your work and do the research to figure out what is a good price range for your genre.

It really is very simple. And then, if you have the price stated clearly, you can do those special one-day sales to see how well your customers can snort.

You set the perceived value of your work.

Do not set it with emotions and fear and self-loathing.

Pretty sure self-loathing is not a principle in business pricing economics. (Except for young writers in fiction. Since new writers gained this control, they have taken self-loathing of their own work into the gutter of pricing. Stop now. Just stop.)

The New Traditional Model of Perceived Value

Here is where things get tough and I will not turn one person's head, but I have to talk about it.

Intellectual property (IP) is what makes up all the pies and cakes in your bakery. Everyone got that?

IP has a value. (Yeah, Dean, we know, we know.)

But alas, you do not know at what level.

Ever wonder why over the last ten years traditional publishing contracts have gone to all-rights for the life of the copyright?

Ever wonder why it is almost impossible now to get books back from traditional publishers once you have sold all rights?

Because IP has a value. Not just a sales value of possible income earned. An accounting value to major corporations.

There are many, many companies now that are buying IP and have no intent of ever marketing it or publishing it or making it into a movie. They simply want the IP.

Yes, your IP. (Your pie, your cake.)

I'll bet you didn't know that there are a ton of major companies out there with the only job, the only reason they exist, is to value IP for other companies.

Don't believe me? Simply Google "IP Valuation" and then do some reading.

THIS PRACTICE HAS ONLY BEEN AROUND FOR A DECADE OR TWO. Yeah, about the time traditional publishers stopped putting in even decent claw-back clauses for your rights and bought everything.

They bought your entire magic pie and they took it out of your store and they know how to value it. They do not care if anything is ever made. They need the value for their bottom lines in the accounting.

Your pie adds value to the big corporation base.

At the moment there are four or five ways that are basic ways that these valuation companies value your IP. But a couple of the sites said there are over 25 other alternative methods.

Trust me, traditional publishing, after grabbing your IP for next to nothing, leaving your bakery with your pie, know all the tricks of making your IP far, far more valuable to their bottom line than what they actually paid.

There is even one method called "Relief from Royalty" that allows the valuation to be made up in case they needed to sell the movie rights, or the translation rights, or whatever. And assuming all those rights did sell in this made-up "arms-length" scenario, that would be the value of your IP.

And did you know one major thing about IP??? It is a property and thus can, under certain circumstances, be depreciated by the corporation.

So they buy your IP for $5,000 because they promised you a movie. They now own it.

They value it under one of the many ways of valuation far, far higher than what they paid and get some major valuation company to sign off on it.

Then they start depreciating it to get the tax deductions on other money coming in. Only one minor way.

Another method is the "Venture Capital Method" which is a name for what I try to get writers to understand about the value of their copyright over the 70 years past death. This method basically values the possible future cash flow OVER THE ASSET'S LIFE. And there is no adjustment to any probability of success. Just a wild guess as to what it might make over its lifetime. Yup.

Your wonderful pie is nothing more than an accounting trick.

(If you want to read one good article about this on the IP Watchdog site, it is here. But do the Google search. It will blow you away.)

Summary

—Never sell all rights. Never let your pie leave your bakery for any reason or any amount of money.

—Research and learn the common indie prices for your books, both paper and electronic. (Ignore traditional publishing prices, as you have just figured out, they sort of don't much care any more.)

—Grow a sense of self-worth that your writing has value. Then treat it as it has value.

How your readers perceive your work is everything in this new world. Start making sure they don't think of your stuff as cheap plastic doomed for the Dollar Store.

Part 2 coming in the next issue.

More WMG Writers' Guides
from all your favorite booksellers
in trade paper and electronic editions.

The First Cold Poker Gang Novel
Available in electronic format or print
at your favorite booksellers.

USA *Today* Bestselling Writer

DEAN WESLEY SMITH

THROUGH THE FOR SALE SIGN

A Bryant Street Story

Strange things always happen on Bryant Street.

Unexplainable things. George Wayne Hooper loves living there.

Former real estate agent, George's talent for reading houses fits the weirdness of Bryant Street.

Another twisted tale of the strange life on the normal-looking Bryant Street.

THROUGH THE FOR SALE SIGN
A Bryant Street Story

GEORGE WAYNE HOOPER stood on the sidewalk staring at the For Sale sign that had just appeared that morning in the dry weeds of what used to be the front lawn of Dot and Dan's home. It had only been a matter of time before the sign would appear. He knew that. Bank notices had been on the door for months.

Today it seemed the house might start to find a new owner. Finally.

Around him the dry air of a Boise fall day was promising to be warm, even though the morning air still had a bite to it. He looked both ways along Bryant Street, the long suburban street turning slightly to the right about seven houses away.

Except for Dot and Dan's traditional three-bedroom ranch house, all the other homes along Bryant Street were well maintained, including his own about twenty houses to the left.

George loved his morning walks after everyone else had left for their regular work. Exactly two miles long, he circled the entire subdivision and walked past every house seven days a week.

He had done that for years since his wife Madge had died, so he knew just about everything that happened on this street. He never talked to anyone about any of it, but he enjoyed knowing.

Very few children lived along Bryant Street and almost always both partners in a home worked. He was the only retired person who lived alone on the street. So he always felt every weekday morning he had the entire subdivision to himself.

Today was Tuesday and no one was home anywhere in sight. The air was still with no wind and the only sounds were some birds around a feeder two houses away and the rumbling of traffic in the distance from the unseen freeway.

George stood not more than five-two with his dress shoes on. But since Madge had died, he never wore any kind of dress clothes. Had no reason to. Mostly he just wore his tan slacks, a tan dress shirt covered by a brown button-down sweater, and tennis shoes.

He and Madge had no children, and at seventy, most of his friends were dead or in homes dying of one thing or another. He figured his morning walks had helped keep him healthy.

When he did happen to run into someone on a weekend, he always smiled and waved and they always smiled and waved back. He was like a light post or a street sign in this subdivision. He was just part of the place, a part that no one noticed unless forced.

And since he made no trouble and made no one actually look at him and ask questions, he got to do what he wanted.

And he honestly liked it that way, especially on mornings like this.

Today, he would finally get a chance to see what exactly happened to Dot and Dan. One day this light-brown home had been just another home he walked past, the next they were gone and the place had been emptied out.

He never saw a moving truck or any packing activity at all. And he hadn't missed a day on his walk.

Very strange.

On Bryant Street, a lot of strange things happened with frightening regularity, but this was one of the strangest.

He had been waiting patiently for the For Sale sign to go up. Now it was here and today was the day, finally, he would get some answers.

Before he retired to take care of Madge as she had been eaten by cancer, he had worked as a real estate agent. He had done it his entire life and he was stunningly good at it, making himself and Madge very rich.

He had discovered when he started into real estate that he had a special talent he never mentioned to anyone, including Madge.

By simply touching a For Sale sign and then going inside the house and touching something in the house, he knew everything about the previous tenants. All of them all the way back to when the building was built.

He had ignored that talent at first, thinking he was going crazy. But the more he researched what he just "knew," the more he came to trust it.

And he decided early on he would never hide anything about a house from any potential buyer. And by being honest with the buyers, he quickly made a reputation for himself as the person to go to when someone wanted to buy a house.

But now, retired, his skill was only for times like this, when his curiosity really wanted to find out what happened in a home.

He looked both ways and then started up the home's sidewalk through the weeds of the front lawn and planter beds.

A realtor lock-box hung on the door as he expected it would. He had kept his real estate license up so he could legally enter the home without getting into any problem.

He took out his cell phone and called the listing agent, identifying himself and saying he wanted to take a quick look at the home on Bryant Street for a client.

The listing agent gave him the lock box combination and he was all set.

He went back to the edge of the street and touched the For Sale sign, then moved up the sidewalk again, trying to walk slowly even though the excitement of the moment was more than he had felt in a year.

He opened the lock box, got the house key and unlocked the front door. He put the key back in the lock box and closed it before stepping inside and closing the front door behind him.

With the slight thump of the door shutting, he had vanished from his morning walk.

The house smelled musty as he had expected it would from being closed up and empty for so long. The blinds were all pulled and the inside was empty and dark.

So what had happened to Dot and Dan? He had never met them, but they had looked so normal the numbers of times he saw them. Both had been in their early thirties or so. Both attractive. No children, but seemingly a lot of friends.

George clicked on the lights in the carpeted living room area.

No furniture remained.

Nothing.

Just an empty expanse of light-blue carpet that showed some stains and a lot of dirt around the ends. A kitchen and dining area was beyond an archway toward the back of the house and a hallway led off to the right to the three bedrooms and two baths.

It was at the moment that he touched the light switch that he knew what had happened to Dot and Dan.

His knees got weak and he had to hold himself up against the wall near the front door.

Dot and Dan had been the third owners of this home. One couple by the name of Swenson had originally built the house and sold it four years later to the Craigs. They had sold it to Dot and Dan five years ago.

And from what George could tell from his vision of previous owners, Dot and Dan had been happy here until one night eight months ago.

It seems Dan had been a jeweler by trade.

George kept his hand pressed against the wall not only for support, but to keep the information flowing from the house to him through his special power. He made himself take deep breaths of the musty air, trying to calm his nerves.

It also seemed that Dan and Dot had been doing a little import business on the side. Importing some cut-rate jewels with questionable backgrounds and reselling them.

When they bought the house, they had done some remodeling and built a full basement under the house. An unpermitted basement that did not show on the original plans.

Only Dot and Dan knew about the basement. It was where they stored what they imported.

George moved away from the entrance and through the empty kitchen toward the garage door. The house had a two-car garage that was completely empty, but George knew that another door led off the back mudroom and down to the basement.

A hidden door behind a small built-in bench and coat racks.

Looking George would have never known the opening was there and there was no sign around the outside of any basement.

But George knew how to open that secret door. He needed to pull on one coat hook while lifting the edge of the bench at the same time.

He started to reach for the bench and the coat hook and then stopped, realizing what he had almost done.

Dot and Dan were down there, in that basement, with all of their furniture.

His vision had told him that three men had visited Dot and Dan, forced them into the hidden basement and killed them. The men had taken all the jewels and spent seven hours that evening moving all the furniture from the home, the clothing, everything, down there, so it would look like Dot and Dan had just suddenly moved away and left the house for the bank.

The last image George had was Dot and Dan's two cars pulling out of the garage, driven by two of the killers just before dawn in March.

No one had found the hidden basement in all the bank inspections and realtor inspections.

No one ever would find that door. No one but George and the three killers even knew it was there.

George walked back toward the front door. He had no idea at all what he should do. No one would believe him if he said he had a special power that told him about the basement.

Maybe he could pretend that Dan and Dot had told him about the hidden basement, but not know how to find it, ask the realtor where it was, have the realtor find the basement and the bodies.

But that would get him answering questions he didn't have answers to. He had never really talked with Dan and Dot.

And he had no client he was looking at the house for.

He had no idea what he should do. The right thing would be to tell the realtor about the missing basement.

But that would change his life, he had no doubt.

He went back out into the growing warmth of the morning and made sure the door was locked behind him. Then he continued on with his walk.

He was back to his home, standing in his own living room, when the solution came to him.

He did some quick research, checked with construction records online, then the bank listing saying the house didn't have a basement.

And then to make sure, he checked the exact date that Dot and Dan had bought the house.

His vision had been right, just as it always had been. They had bought the house just a few weeks after Madge died.

With shaking hands, George picked up the phone and called his old company.

Stan, the owner of the real estate firm was two years older than George and still working, often saying they would pry his cold dead fingers off the business and not a moment before. Numbers of times since Madge died Stan had offered George his position back.

George had always appreciated the gesture, but had said no. He didn't need the money and until this morning had enjoyed his daily walks and his routines.

When Stan came on the line, he was darned happy to hear from George, again offering his old job back.

"Can't do it," George said, "but got a house listing, bank owned, that just popped up on my street today. Thought it might be something you would want to latch onto so I gave it a look-see. Found some strange things. Or better put, didn't find some things. For example, I didn't find the basement."

Stan laughed. "George, you know you always had a way with houses. But sure the age isn't getting to you. Basements are the things you go down stairs to find."

George laughed. "No stairs."

"So how do you know the place is supposed to have a basement?" Stan asked.

"I started taking walks around this subdivision right after Madge died," George said. "On a number of those walks I watched the previous owners take out enough dirt through their garage in trucks to build a basement under the house."

"Okay, so they hid the stairs. And what's the problem with that?" Stan asked.

"No basement listed. Nothing permitted or recorded. Bank doesn't have it priced for a basement either. And I couldn't find any door to a basement. But if there is a basement down there, that house is a steal at the price they have on it. Might want to go give it a look."

"Damn, appreciate that," Stan said.

George smiled. Even at seventy-three, Stan never missed a good deal when it came along.

"I got a friend with some of that new equipment that he can see through walls," Stan said, "and down into the ground to find pipes and such. We'll haul that along."

"Let me know what you find," George said. "Drove me nuts not being able to find that basement door this morning."

"Sure you don't want your job back?" Stan asked.

"Only if you give me your job," George said, laughing.

Stan laughed as well, thanked him, and hung up.

George made himself stay on routine for the rest of the day, eating lunch at his normal place downtown, taking another walk around the homes in the North End of Boise along the beautiful tree-lined streets, then going home to cook himself dinner and watch television.

He went out for his normal walk the next morning at his normal time. Two police cars were in front of Dot and Dan's house and the entire yard was taped off as a crime scene.

It seemed that Dot and Dan had been found.

He stood around watching the police come in and out of the home for a few minutes, then continued on with his walk.

It was a nice morning and there was yet another house empty on Bryant Street he was waiting for a For Sale sign to go up.

That always excited him because on Bryant Street, there was just no way of knowing what a house would tell him about its owners.

Betty Spencer dislikes nerds. Especially nerds with bad teeth.

Superficial describes Betty perfectly. Proudly superficial, actually.

Nerd extraordinaire, Brad Fanthorpe asks Betty for a date. Unthinkable.

But Brad understands Betty perfectly.

A superficially funny story about being superficial.

SMILE

Day One Lunch

"I'D WALK CHAMELEON miles for one of your smiles."

Betty Spencer wiped her hands on her brown uniform and looked up over the Faster-Than-Yours Burgers and Things cash register at the nerd standing at the head of the line. He stood no more than five-six, had a face full of bad zits, and wore plaid pants.

She couldn't believe the plaid pants.

"Can I help you?" she asked, forcing on her best Faster-Than-Yours training smile. Being the best-looking woman employee, she always got all the weird men in her line. Half the time they wouldn't even look up from her chest.

And the few gorgeous men who did come in wouldn't even notice her because of the bag-like brown uniform they made her wear.

Working here was just a bitch.

"I'd walk chameleon miles for one of your smiles," the nerd said again. Then he stuck out a stubby-fingered hand. "I'm Brad. Brad Fanthorpe. I've been in here every day this summer. I just love it when you smile."

Betty glanced quickly over her shoulder at where her supervisor stood over-salting the French fries. He might look her way at any moment. She would have to be careful how she handled this guy. She was already on the supervisor's shit list for making a pass at the cook. How the hell was she supposed to know that the cook was as gay as the supervisor and they'd been living together for the past three months.

Working here was an absolute bitch.

She turned back to the nerd, let the official work smile drain down into what she really felt, then looked him right in the eye and said, "That's nice. Now, what can I get for you?"

"Oh, nothing to eat," the nerd said. "I just wanted to ask you to a movie this evening."

The nerd smiled real big.

Betty's stomach turned just like it had the first time she had tasted a Faster-Than-Yours burger. The nerd's teeth looked like they hadn't been brushed in

six months and she could smell his breath clear across the counter.

"No thanks," she said. "I'm busy. And besides, I only go out with men over six feet tall."

"Oh, no problem at all," he said. "Thanks."

He bowed slightly, then turned and walked away.

As the next customer, an overweight man with two kids moved up in front of her, Betty glanced over at her boss. He was still doing rude things to the French fries and hadn't seen what had happened.

Thank God. She got in enough trouble on her own without having some jerk cause her even more.

Working here was sure a bitch. She forced on her smile for the dirty-faced kid in front of her.

Day One Afternoon

"I'D WALK CHAMELEON** miles for one of your smiles."

Betty glanced up from the order of Itsy-Bitsy Chicken Parts she had been trying to choke down for lunch. The nerd was back, standing beside her table, smiling his rotten-teeth smile.

"Remember me," he said. "I'm Brad Fanthorpe. I was in earlier."

He stuck out his hand again.

Betty ignored the hand.

"Yeah, I remember you," she said. How anyone could ever forget someone with breath like his was beyond her. She swore it was shriveling up her already tiny Chicken Parts lunch.

"Well," he said, indicating his legs. "What do you think? I'm six feet, two

50

inches tall now. I had to buy new pants, but it was worth it if you will go out with me tomorrow night."

Betty looked at his pants. They looked like the same plaid pants he'd had on earlier, only these still had a price sticker on one side.

She had to admit, though, he did look taller. Some sort of lifts, or maybe a trick.

"I'm busy tomorrow night, too," she said. "And besides, not only are all of my dates over six feet tall, they all look like Bruce Springsteen."

"Oh, no problem," he said. "Thanks." Again, he bowed slightly and headed for the door.

Betty picked up a Chicken Part, then dropped it back into its box.

All she had wanted was to earn a little spending money for her junior year at the University. What the hell had she done to deserve this job?

Day One Evening

"I'D WALK CHAMELEON miles for one of your smiles."

Betty had just left the employee entrance and was trying to unlock her car. She had noticed the guy standing beside the car next to hers, but she hadn't paid much attention. Now she spun and looked right into the face of Bruce Springsteen.

"Holy shit!" she said. She didn't know whether to run like hell away from him, or move closer for a better look.

She ended up just standing there and staring. And the more she stared, the more she realized it wasn't Bruce after all.

"Hi. Remember me? I'm Brad Fanthorpe."

Just like the times earlier in the day, he stuck out his hand and moved toward her.

Just like before, there was no way she was going to touch his hand.

"Well? What do you think? Will you go out with me three nights from now?"

He smiled, showing her his rotted teeth again.

"How? I mean, why— No, what I meant to say is that is some great mask."

Having a tall, Bruce Springsteen look-a-like standing in front of her was making her nervous, even if he did have bad teeth and wore plaid pants. He was just so damned good looking.

"It's no mask," he said. "I changed just for you."

"Sure you did," Betty said. Even if he was good looking, this guy was just too weird.

She went back to unlocking her car.

"No," the guy said. "I did. Really."

Betty had the car door open now. She felt safer, so she turned and faced him. Better to get it over with now instead of having him come back while she was working tomorrow.

"Is that what all this 'chameleon mile' shit is about? I thought chameleons were lizards."

"They are," he said. "They can change their colors to blend in with their surroundings. I've spent the last three years at the University working on a way to do much more than chameleons can do."

"And just how do you do it?" Betty asked with as much sarcasm as she could put in her voice. "Drink a secret formula?"

"On no," he said. "Nothing like that. It's a combination of a special cream and metaphysical techniques."

"I don't believe this shit," Betty said and started to climb into her car.

"Wait! What about the date?"

"Tell you what," Betty said. "If you can give yourself not only Bruce's shoulders and chest, but his ass, I'll go out with you. Deal?"

She slammed her door, backed out, and drove off with him still standing there in the parking lot.

What a day. They didn't pay her enough for this job. Not by a million dollars.

Day Two Breakfast

THE NEXT MORNING, Betty had just finished serving her last order of Pigs-in-a-Bun and was starting to clean up to get ready for the lunch rush.

Suddenly Debbie, the blonde-haired giggle machine who worked at the cash register beside Betty's, let out a scream, "It's him! It's really him!"

Then Debbie sighed real loud and slumped to the floor, giving her head a sound crack on the just-mopped tiles.

Betty looked up.

Bruce Springsteen was walking right at her.

"Holy shit!" Betty said and stepped back away from the counter.

It couldn't be Bruce.

But it also couldn't be the nerd.

"Well?" Bruce said in the nerd's voice. "What do you think?"

He held up his hands and turned around, showing Betty his ass.

"Not bad, huh?"

"Holy shit!" Betty said again as she looked him up and down. He still had on the plaid pants, but somehow, on Bruce's body, they now looked great.

Sexy.

His button-down shirt looked two sizes too small and Betty could see dark brown hair on his chest.

"How about that date now?" Bruce asked.

"You want to go out with her?" the supervisor said as he walked up and stood beside Betty. "I'm sure Mr. Springsteen tha—"

"I'm not Bruce Springsteen," Bruce said. "I'm Brad Fanthorpe."

He stuck out his hand for the supervisor to shake.

"Anything you say," the supervisor said softly as he took the offered hand and shook it as if he never wanted to let go.

Betty tore her gaze off of Bruce's chest and glanced around.

A crowd was starting to gather. All the girls were now standing behind her and some of the breakfast customers were whispering to each other and pointing.

"Excuse me, Sir," Betty said. "Would it be possible that I take my break now?"

The supervisor glanced at her without letting go of Bruce's hand. "I don't—"

"That would be great if you'd let her just have five minutes," Bruce said and smiled at the supervisor.

"Oh, of course," the supervisor said and let go of Bruce's hand. "But just five minutes."

Betty nodded and quickly ducked around the end of the counter and led Bruce to the farthest booth.

She just couldn't believe this was happening. Her eyes told her that she was with Bruce Springsteen, but her mind said it was still the nerd.

Only there was no way that it could be either.

Someone was playing a practical joke on her and it wasn't damn funny. It was going to get her fired.

"All right," she said after they were both seated. "What's this all about?"

"Just trying to get a date with you," he said. "You said you were busy the next two nights, so how about Friday night?"

"Just hang on a minute. First off, I want to know just how you did this. I mean, what kind of trick—no, I mean, who are you? Hell, I don't know what I mean."

"Don't you remember?" he asked. "I told you yesterday. I'm Brad Fanthorpe and I changed to get a date with you. You did say you wouldn't go out with me unless I was over six feet tall and looked like Bruce Springsteen. So I used the picture on his latest album to make myself look exactly like him. Neat, huh?"

He smiled and Betty could see his bad teeth.

He closed his mouth and she was left staring into Bruce Springsteen's face.

What the hell was she going to do now?

She reached across the table and touched the side of his face, then squeezed his arm.

It felt like real flesh and she couldn't see any makeup. Maybe, just maybe, the impossible was true and this guy really could change into whoever he wanted. That didn't make him Bruce Springsteen. He was still just the nerd that had come in yesterday.

Only now he was damn good looking.

"How long does this—this effect last?"

Bruce shook his head. "I don't know. For all I know, it may be permanent, at least until I change it to something different."

"Oh," was all Betty could say.

Now that she had let herself start to accept that what he was saying might be true, her mind was racing with all the possibilities. It would mean that anyone could look young anytime they wanted. It would mean that no one ever would have to be ugly. Or deformed.

It would mean that she could look like anyone she wanted to look like.

This guy's invention would change the world.

"Have you told anyone about this invention?" Betty asked.

"Just a few others," he said. "I just got it to work three days ago."

"If you gave me some of this cream," Betty said, "would I be able to change, too?"

Bruce looked puzzled. "I suppose so. It might take me a few years to train you in the metaphysical trances involved, but I suppose you could do it. I really haven't thought all the implications of this through, yet. But I suppose anyone could be taught."

His gaze held hers and then he smiled.

"But why would you want to. I think you're very beautiful just the way you are."

Betty could feel her face getting red and slightly hot. It wasn't very often that she had a man as good looking as he was compliment her, even if he had been a nerd the day before.

"Two years?" she asked after a moment of silence. "Why so long?"

"It would take at least that long to train your mind," he said. "The cream is only an enhancer. It's the mind that has the power to change the body. You'd have to learn to tap into that power and control it."

"Oh," Betty said, again. That didn't sound real hopeful. She'd never been any good at that sort of strong concentration. It usually took everything she could do just to keep her mind on one subject for an hour class.

"Now, what about the date?" Bruce asked. "I was thinking we could catch a movie."

Betty glanced around at the counter. Not only were all the girls staring in her direction, but also the cook, the supervisor, and most of the customers. They all literally looked as if they were drooling. If she didn't go out with Bruce, or Brad, or whatever his name was, there was no doubt he would have absolutely no trouble getting anyone else in the place to go.

She looked back at him. He really did seem like a nice guy. Definitely smart. Maybe after the first date, she could get him to do something about his teeth.

"All right," she said. "But how about tonight? I'm free after all."

He slowly shook his head. "I really can't," he said, giving her his Bruce Springsteen serious look that made her hot all over. "I've got a date with Judy from the pizza place down the street."

Betty could feel her stomach starting to twist. "How about tomorrow night, then?"

He shook his head again. "Tomorrow I'm going out with Ann from the Milkshake Palace. Sorry, but it will have to be Friday. Would that be all right? I really would like to go out with you. Just this once."

Just this once echoed around and around in her head as she heard herself say, "Friday would be nice."

"Great," he said and stood. "I'll let you get back to work, now. I'll pick you up here after work on Friday. Okay?"

"Fine," she said, softly.

Then she looked up at him. "Wait. Would you tell me something before you go?"

"Sure."

"You said there were only a few others that knew about your invention. Are they the other girls?"

"That's right," he said. "Why?"

"Oh," Betty said. "I was just wondering if your other dates liked Bruce Springsteen, too."

Bruce laughed and patted her on the shoulder. "Nope. Judy is attracted to men who look like Paul McCartney and Ann likes soldiers. Francis, down at the sporting goods store gets real excited over jocks, and Cathy in my chemistry class literally drools over professor types. Everyone has different tastes. Lucky for me, I can change real fast. I'll see you Friday."

He patted her lightly on the shoulder again and headed for the door with literally everyone in the Faster-Than-Yours Burgers and Things watching him.

Betty laid her head down on the table, closed her eyes, and tried to calm the jealousy twisting her stomach into hard knots.

Four other women.

Lucky for him he could change fast?

How could she have been so stupid?

His words, "Just this once" echoed around in her mind.

One date.

Four other girls.

If she wanted to see him again, Friday was really going to have to be something.

That was the answer. She would make Friday a date to remember.

She stood and headed back for the counter, already planning the evening. She'd show that nerd a move or two.

Then, maybe on their second date, she'd get him to do something about those teeth.

USA *Today* Bestselling Writer

DEAN WESLEY SMITH

*Four good friends
and the habit of living.*

HABIT

Charles lived as part of the regulars in the Haven Bar. Everyone knew what he drank, when he came in, what he laughed at.

And he loved discussions. So on the night he starts the discussion of habits, nothing seems wrong.

But we all live the sum of our habits. And when those habits break, nothing ever remains the same.

For my friend Bill. Miss the habit of talking with you old friend.

HABIT

"Is a person dead whose entire existence is nothing more than one habit after another, or does death only come with the breaking of the habit of living?"
—J. Michael Grove

ONE

"HABIT. YOU EVER notice how habit drives a person?"

I jumped, banged my knee under the bar, and sloshed scotch in a cold stream down the back of my hand.

"Damn it!" I swung around to face Edward "Charles" Meredith. "Would you make some noise when you come in?"

Charles just laughed. He and I were part of what we called "The Gang," five regulars of the Haven Lounge who unofficially met four times a week to do nothing but talk, drink, and just feel like belonging.

Our home, the Haven, was one of those places that stood like an island in the center of a rough lake. I have to say, the name of the place sort of fit.

Year after year its wood floors, glass-ringed bar, and many plants had survived the time-lashed winds of change that ripped down the surrounding buildings and jumbled them into new shapes. Only the color of the regular's hair and the size of the plants ticked off the passage of the years inside that large wooden front door.

The gang was an odd group by any standards.

Shipley, the tallest and youngest member at forty, had figured out that he had drank over sixteen thousand beers in the twenty years he had been a part of the group. Charles claimed over twenty thousand and everyone kidded him the extra four thousand showed.

Back in the early years, Charles carried his weight like a football player fresh off the field. His arms and chest intimidated the loudest of arguments.

I still remember the first night he came in. He was new in town, new to teaching at the University, and mad at the world from an ugly divorce.

He wore an expensive gray suit, a loud white and gray tie, and a gray fedora. That night he laid the hat directly in front of the end stool, hung his suit jacket like a carcass of an animal across the back of the stool, and yelled for a beer. Over the years, he stopped wearing the suits, but the hat never failed to fill the inside edge of the bar in front of the end stool.

Of all the gang, Charles felt the winds of time the hardest. What was left of his hair had turned completely silver. His massive chest had pulled in on itself like a potato going bad in the hot afternoon sun and the strength of his yell had diminished along with the length of his stride from the door to the bar.

But his mind stayed clear. He had slowly accepted the loss of his physical power, but refused to do anything but grow with his mind. Every week he had a new topic he was concerned with.

It looked like "Habit" might be the topic for this week.

"We're all driven by habit," Charles said. "Do you realize that? Have you ever stopped and thought about habits? You haven't. I can tell. Let me give you an example. What am I going to order now?"

"A glass of Bud?" I said. When Charles got this worked up it was always better to just go along.

"Exactly," he said, slapping his hand down on the bar. "My point exactly. How did you know that?"

I shrugged. "Not a real tough question. You've been drinking Bud for over twenty years."

"Habit," he said, again slapping his hand down on the bar. I guess I was supposed to see his point clear as a bell. I didn't. But that too wasn't at all unusual.

Frank, the owner of the Haven and main bartender on the nights the gang was in, slid a beer and napkin in front of Charles.

"How'd you know what I wanted?" Charles demanded of Frank.

Frank looked over at me and I shrugged, letting him know it was just Charles starting into his weekly topic. Frank knew exactly how to handle Charles. He'd been the bartender almost every night the gang had met. He was as much a part of the gang as anyone.

"You always drink Bud," Frank said.

Charles pointed a thin finger at me. "See what I mean?"

"Everyone has habits," I said. "So what's so unusual about that?"

"The length, man," Charles said. "The incredible lengths that we'll all carry our habits to. Who knows, maybe even beyond death."

He turned slowly back straight on the stool, facing his drink, and wrapped both hands around his beer.

I had no idea what the hell he was driving at. But I had little shivers running up and down my spine that was for sure. Frank didn't like the sounds of the topic either, but we couldn't get Charles to talk any more.

That was always the way he was. When he turned back to face his drink, the discussion was over for the moment. But I had no doubt we would be talking about habits a lot more during the week.

A few minutes later I was called to the other end of the bar for one of Shipley's famous jokes and didn't see when Charles left.

TWO

THE NEXT NIGHT I again had my back to Charles's stool when he said, "Habits sure are fascinating, aren't they?"

I jumped again. This week must be his week to sneak into the Haven and scare me.

"Damn it, Charles," I said. "How'd you get in here without me seeing you?"

Charles laughed. "Maybe a new habit?"

"I hope not. My heart couldn't stand it."

Frank slipped a beer in front of Charles.

"Evening," Frank said. "Didn't see you come in."

Charles shrugged. "Maybe I'm really not here."

Both Frank and I laughed at that one as Charles went on. "What would happen if one night I didn't bring my hat?"

He spun the old fedora on the slick surface of the wood bar.

"I suppose we'd all live," I said. "But I'd miss it."

"So would I," Charles said. "But it wouldn't be the end of everything, would it?"

I shook my head. "I don't see what you're driving at."

"It has occurred to me that life is nothing but linked habits. The more settled you become, the older you are, the more habits you collect. Then suddenly you realize that you have gone an entire day and done nothing but one habit after another. I came to that realization Sunday."

"You think we all do that?"

Charles nodded. "At least all of us here do. Tell me when you always do your bookkeeping down at the store."

I owned Taylor's Grocery down on Seventh. I called it the biggest independent in the state. "About two," I said.

"What do you do directly before that?" Charles asked. "And directly after?"

It didn't take much thought on my part to give him that point. I did exactly the same thing every day.

"All right, you have me there. But I still don't see what you're driving at."

"Neither do I," Frank said.

Charles twisted his full glass of beer. "I think habit is like aging. It is one of the body's ways of working toward death. The older you get, the more habit-riddled you become. And the more uncomfortable it is to break the patterns."

"You're saying the young don't have habits?" Frank asked.

"The truly young don't," Charles said. "They constantly change and explore everything new. That's why those of us who acquire habits like gray hairs are bothered by the young. We don't like those with the courage to change."

"You want to switch stools?" I asked.

He laughed. "No, I'm afraid it's far too late for that now."

He turned back to face his beer, the signal that the discussion was over.

Again that night, I didn't see him leave.

THREE

WEDNESDAY NIGHT STARTED with the craziest question I had heard in a long time. I was still damp from my fight through the rain and had my first scotch about half put away when Shipley ambled down the bar toward me.

"You seen Charles lately?" he asked.

That question was usually reserved for a time when one of the gang had been missing for a few days. I was sure Shipley had seen Charles last night.

"He's been here the last two nights," I said.

I was half expecting some sort of practical joke, like Charles sneaking in behind me again.

But Shipley looked honestly puzzled. "No he hasn't. I haven't seen him in here since last Thursday."

I always get this cramping feeling in my stomach when I know I'm about to face something I don't like. Dentists do

that to me every time. Death does the same thing. Right now cramps were having a parade through my stomach.

"I talked to him last night and Monday," I said. "Ask Frank. He served him."

Big Wayne turned and looked at me. Big Wayne always sat on my left at the bar and seldom looked away from his drink. He drove beer truck and almost never said any more than three words at a time. But when he said something, everyone listened. It was just the way he was.

"He hasn't been here," Big Wayne said.

"Frank!" I called out. Frank turned from talking to one of the waitresses and moved down to where we were talking.

"Has Charles been here the last few nights?"

Frank nodded. "Both Monday and last night. Why?"

"See?" I said, but it didn't stop the cramping in my stomach.

"He hasn't been here," Big Wayne said.

Chills.

All over.

Damn I hated that.

Frank's face lost some of its color.

Shipley and I looked at each other, then at Big Wayne.

Talk about habit. When Big Wayne made a statement like that, you didn't question it. He was never wrong. Not once in twenty years had he been wrong when he repeated something.

"But I talked to him," I said. My voice sounded lame even to me.

"I'll find out for sure," Shipley said as he headed for the phone in the back storage room. My gut said there wasn't going to be an answer.

I stared down into my scotch thinking about what Charles had said the past two nights.

He had lectured me on habit. On the fact that I had expected him to be sitting there.

Maybe that had been his point.

If it was, I didn't want to know it.

Shipley stepped from the storage room door and shook his head.

Big Wayne and I grabbed our coats and Shipley was right behind us on the way out the front door.

We found Charles slumped in his favorite reading chair.

The coroner said it had been a massive heart attack sometime Sunday. He hadn't lasted for more than a minute.

FOUR

THE NEXT MONDAY, I thought I saw Charles's hat sitting on the bar beside me.

I knew it couldn't be there. We had buried him, so of course his hat wasn't there.

But over the next few months I caught glimpses of it out of the corner of my eye and more than once turned to ask him a question or throw him a one-liner.

Charles's stool stayed empty for the rest of the year. Even during the busiest of the gang nights, that one empty stool would remain an island in the storm.

But I'm not so sure it was empty. Not after everything Charles had said about habits.

I switched to drinking tonics for a while, then to beer. But it felt uncomfortable and I ended up back with the scotch. I'm sure Charles would have laughed.

It took a long time for those of us in the gang to break the habit of Charles being there and replace it with new people, new habits.

It's sad the way it worked.

For Charles, real death didn't come when his heart gave out. It came when those of us who cared lost the habit of him being around.

~

Some Classic Dean Wesley Smith Stories
Available at your favorite booksellers.

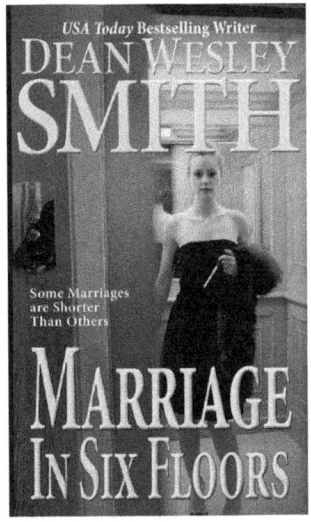

DEATH TAKES A DIAMOND

A MARY JO ASSASSIN NOVEL

DEAN WESLEY SMITH

USA TODAY BESTSELLING AUTHOR

When a contract comes in on another assassin, Mary Jo must discover why. Assassins don't kill assassins.

With four ancient-order assassins working together, anything becomes possible.

Sex, murder, and diamonds. And pretty much in that order.

Only Mary Jo Assassin can deliver all three with a smile and a vodka orange juice drink in her hand.

DEATH TAKES A DIAMOND
A Mary Jo Assassin Novel

Dedicated and with a special thanks to Allyson!

PART ONE
A Problem Solved

ONE

MARY JO USUALLY loved mornings. The fresh promise of a new day at hand, the savory taste of freshly brewed coffee, the smell of eggs and ham.

This morning wasn't that much different from her normal mornings. She went through her daily ritual of showering and getting dressed. Jean, Mary Jo's partner, lover, and roommate, didn't much go for mornings, so she normally slept in and it wasn't until hours later that Jean usually crawled out of bed.

But this morning, because Mary Jo was at a critical point on a job, Jean got up and cooked her breakfast. They had learned that working together was so much more fun than working alone, so they shared everything, and Mary Jo was glad they did.

Especially today.

There was something about this job Mary Jo had been hired to do that bothered both her and Jean and neither of them could put their finger on the problem.

Today they would find out what exactly was happening.

Mary Jo came out of the New York City penthouse apartment's main bathroom and into the modern kitchen where the sound of ham sizzling greeted her along with the thick, rich smell of freshly brewed coffee.

She had just entered heaven.

Early morning sun streaming in the large windows near the dining nook made it even nicer as below them the wonderful city started to wake up.

Mary Jo loved how Jean normally looked in the mornings, her blond hair pulled back, her perfect body tucked into a thin cotton robe. But this morning Jean had gotten dressed in Levi's and a silk blouse and tennis shoes, her working clothes. She had actually gotten up ahead of Mary Jo, which in their two years together had almost never happened.

Mary Jo thought Jean the most beautiful woman Mary Jo had ever seen. Jean said the same about Mary Jo. There was no doubt they were a striking couple from all the looks they got when they went out in public.

Jean, at five-three was two inches taller than Mary Jo. Jean had blonde hair and bright green eyes, while Mary Jo had short very dark-brown hair and deep dark-brown eyes. Mary Jo often wore black wigs and it suited her fine.

What Mary Jo loved was how they fit in each other's arms perfectly. In fact, last night, they had spent an hour in each other's arms naked in the hot tub, sipping wonderful vodka orange juices and going over every detail of Mary Jo's job today.

That was her idea of the ideal way to work.

She loved high quality vodka and fresh-squeezed orange juice. That simple drink would lift anyone's mood. And it certainly did hers most every night.

Luckily, Jean loved the drink as much as Mary Jo did.

She and Jean were professional assassins, and both had done that job for over a thousand years, but as best they could figure, Mary Jo was about a hundred years older than Jean.

Neither one of them could imagine doing anything else but being an assassin.

But this last job Mary Jo had been hired to do just bothered them both, and over the centuries they had learned to listen carefully to that gut sense that something was wrong.

They both thought they knew.

Today, they were going to find out what was bothering them exactly.

Mary Jo hugged Jean from behind as Jean stood at the stove, then went and poured herself a cup of coffee.

Jean already had one for herself on the kitchen table that looked out over a garden area on the roof and the city beyond.

Mary Jo sat and took a sip of the wonderful flavor, then watched Jean move as she cooked. By the way she was moving, it was clear to Mary Jo that Jean was a little worried about the job today.

The job, on the surface, had appeared simple.

Mary Jo had been hired through normal channels by a man named J.T. Sones. He went by Tate, a multi-millionaire head of an information conglomerate that had a good fifty companies under its umbrella.

Mary Jo had received the standard one million up front and would get two million on completion. The job was to kill a woman by the name of Bonnie Malak.

But after two months of looking, Mary Jo could see no connection between Malak and Sones. No business, no past love affair, nothing.

The two had never crossed paths as far as Mary Jo and Jean could tell.

What bothered Mary Jo most was that Bonnie Malak looked like an assassin herself. Short, in shape, clearly in no need of money, living alone just off Broadway in a penthouse apartment. She moved like an assassin and seemed to have few friends and no enemies, the perfect way an assassin lived.

She also seemed to have a history under the Malak name that felt a little too perfect in places.

Tate Sones, on the other hand, had made many enemies over the years. He stood six-foot-one, had the body of a thirty-year-old, even though he was fifty, clearly colored his hair, and clearly exercised. And he acted like a jerk to most people. There were a lot of reasons to want Sones dead, but no reason to want Malak dead.

And that bothered Mary Jo and Jean.

When they had told a third assassin friend of theirs, Susan, she had thought the same thing. Susan lived about eight blocks away and the three of them had worked a number of jobs together.

They trusted each other.

Susan was going to help today as well.

So today they would all find out exactly what was happening. And why. Mary Jo had no problem killing anyone. It was what she had done for more than a thousand years.

But she had always tried to make sure she killed the right person.

Bonnie Malak did not seem to be the right person.

TWO

THE FIRST PART of the plan had gone like clockwork. Mary Jo bumped into Tate Sones "accidently" as he came out of his 5th Avenue apartment elevator into the underground parking of his building.

She had been going in and pretended to trip on the edge of the glass airlock door leading to the elevators.

Sones had caught her, made some comment about she needed to be careful little lady, copped a feel of one of her boobs while helping her, and then went on.

The accident allowed her to stick him lightly with a small amount of a very powerful drug that would knock him out in about thirty seconds.

He made it to his Mercedes sedan, got behind the wheel and passed out. Since his door was closed and his windows tinted, no security cameras could see that.

Earlier, Susan had managed to get into the car without any security seeing her and was waiting in the back seat of the car. She quickly pulled him over into the back seat, then climbed into the driver's seat and put on a chauffeur-style cap even though Sones seldom used a chauffeur in his own car, only in limos. She got the car out of the building just as a normal driver would.

Jean was to meet Susan in the underground parking of an apartment they had rented just for this day and take Sones up to the apartment and tie him up in one bedroom.

Mary Jo's next job was to get Bonnie Malak to the same apartment.

They had all figured out, after watching Bonnie for some time, the best way would be to just level with her and invite her.

Mary Jo, Jean, and Susan were sure Bonnie was an assassin, but short of talking with her, there was no way to know. There certainly wasn't a membership number or something. Assassins were all trained by an ancient order and worked on their own, for the most part.

So in the preparation for today, all three of them had made sure they had watched Bonnie a number of times in an obvious way that an assassin would pick up on if she was good.

As they had watched her, Bonnie had become a creature of habit and would have been an easy target for Mary Jo. Bonnie sat at the same time every morning in the window seat of a deli three blocks from her apartment. A simple sniper shot from a nearby apartment window would have done the trick.

Mary Jo was fairly certain that Bonnie would know that.

Bonnie was a strikingly beautiful woman about Mary Jo's age. She had bright green eyes, red-tinted short hair, and freckles across the bridge of her nose.

Mary Jo went into the deli and ordered a cup of black coffee at the counter without looking at Bonnie. The place smelled wonderful of fresh-made bread combined with a rich, thick smell of bacon. When she took her coffee over to the table, she

was actually surprised at the power and beauty of Bonnie up close.

"Is this seat taken?" Mary Jo asked.

Bonnie looked up and smiled. "For you, it is always available."

Bonnie indicated Mary Jo should pull out the chair and sit across from her in the window.

Most of the people walking by outside were on the way to work. The day was going to be a beautiful spring day with the snows and cold of winter now forgotten.

"I'm Mary Jo," Mary Jo said, holding out her hand.

"Bonnie," the green-eyed woman said, smiling. "But you already know that."

"I do," Mary Jo said, nodding.

"You three have been watching me now for four months, you for longer," Bonnie said. "I've been wondering why, actually."

"You're a target of a contract," Mary Jo said simply. "We wanted to let you know we were there to see what you would do."

Bonnie nodded. "Thanks for not filling the contract just yet. Can I ask who took it out on me?"

Mary Jo was impressed that Bonnie was taking the news so calmly. Chances are inside she wasn't calm, but on the outside she was doing what any trained assassin would do and not show any emotion. And also, chances are, she had figured it was something like this.

"J.T. Sones," Mary Jo said. "He goes by Tate."

Bonnie slowly shook her head. "No memory of anyone by that name."

"We didn't think so," Mary Jo said. "We could find no connection at all. We have Tate Sones under wraps. Would you like to meet him, get to the bottom of all this, before we decide what to do with him."

"I would love to," Bonnie said, nodding. "Thank you."

The two of them headed out of the deli and up the street. Mary Jo knew that in disguises, Jean and Susan were both watching her every move. She couldn't see them, but she knew they were there.

The three of them did not take any chances that didn't need to be taken.

After three blocks of walking in silence through the morning crowds, about a half block from the rented apartment, Bonnie turned to Mary Jo. "You are being very trusting of me."

"Why would you say that?" Mary Jo asked.

"I don't see the two others that helped you."

Mary Jo laughed. "You are not supposed to see us unless we want you to see us."

"I had heard rumors you three were that good," Bonnie said, nodding.

Mary Jo didn't much like that she had a reputation among assassins. But she liked that she was known for being good at her job.

After doing it for over a thousand years, she should be good at it. Otherwise, she would have been dead a long time ago.

THREE

MARY JO LET Bonnie into the two-bedroom apartment on the fifth floor of the walk-up. The buildings next door were so much taller and so close, little natural light could get into the place.

And the furniture was 1960s beat-up. There was even a bottle candle on one end table that had been lit so many times

a black circle had formed on the ceiling above it.

The place had a cloying smell of far too much pot and cigarettes.

Mary Jo let Bonnie enter first.

Bonnie glanced around and nodded. "I like what you did with the place."

Mary Jo smiled and let the door stand open as Jean came through behind her.

"This is Jean," Mary Jo said.

"Wonderful meeting you, Bonnie," Jean said, smiling. "Wow, anyone ever tell you that you are a real stunner?"

"Wow, you are right about that," Susan said, coming in behind Jean. "I'm Susan."

Bonnie smiled at Susan. "You're not so bad yourself."

Mary Jo was pretty convinced that Susan actually blushed a little.

The four of them went into the kitchen. The counters were old and needed repair, a couple of the empty cabinets had lost their doors, and there was a square wooden table to one side.

Bonnie sat down on one metal kitchen chair and Susan sat across from her while Jean and Mary Jo remained standing. Mary Jo could feel a little tension, but not as much as she had expected.

Jean pulled out a cell phone and quickly dialed a number. Then she said, "Freyja Mist."

Mary Jo knew that Jean was calling the ancient order of assassins. She just gave them her assassin name. The order didn't even have a name, but it had recruited all of them way back in time and trained them. It still kept track of all its members. Mary Jo had not contacted them in sixty years, but Jean had no problem calling them when information was needed.

Jean waited, then nodded. "We think we are talking with another member of the order who has been targeted by a client. Can you confirm that this person is an assassin or not?"

"Your name?" Jean asked Bonnie after a moment.

"Sunshine MorningBee," Bonnie said.

Mary Jo knew that the name meant that Bonnie was a younger member of the order, clearly recruited in just the last few hundred years or so.

Jean repeated the name and listened, then nodded and said thank you and hung up the phone.

"Confirmed," Jean said to Mary Jo.

Mary Jo reached down into a cabinet where they had stored a laptop and pulled it out and opened it on the table in front of Bonnie. "So this is the man who is tied up and still out cold in the bedroom."

Mary Jo showed Bonnie a picture of Tate Sones.

Bonnie shook her head. "Never seen him before, nor do I know the name."

Mary Jo ran through Sones' company dealings here in New York and again Bonnie just shook her head no.

"I was in Chicago before finishing a job and heading here."

Then Mary Jo put up a picture of Sones' wife, Holly. She was a short, attractive woman with black hair and dark eyes.

"Oh, shit," Bonnie said, glancing around at the three of them. "I had a wonderful affair with her about a year ago. It lasted for two months and she said her husband was getting suspicious so she broke it off. She said her name was Gretchen Hunt. I knew she was married, but didn't care that much. She was a great time, if you know what I mean."

"Gretchen Hunt is actually Holly Sones," Mary Jo said.

Susan turned the computer so she could see the picture of Gretchen Hunt

Sones. Then Susan looked right at Bonnie. "Think she would be up for a threesome?"

This time it was Bonnie's turn to slightly blush. But then she smiled and said, "Never hurts to ask."

Susan just smiled back and Mary Jo could tell that Susan and Bonnie were making a real connection.

Mary Jo glanced at Jean who just smiled and raised an eyebrow.

"So husband wants to kill wife's lover," Bonnie said. "Gretchen was a wild one. I wonder how many other former loves of Gretchen he has killed?"

"I suppose we could ask him," Mary Jo said, glancing at her watch. "He should be waking up about now."

"I would love to," Bonnie said. Then she looked at Mary Jo. "I know we follow our contracts and all that, but any chance I can buy my way out of the one you have on me?"

Susan, Jean, and Mary Jo all laughed. "We never go against another assassin for any reason."

Now Available
from all your favorite booksellers in trade paper and electronic editions.

Bonnie seemed actually relieved. "I thought I remembered that in my training and that was why I trusted you would come to me to tell me why you were all following me."

"You trusted right," Susan said, smiling at Bonnie and turning her toward the bedroom. "We work alone, we work together, but we never target each other."

"I've never worked with another assassin in three hundred years of doing this," Bonnie said.

"Well," Susan said, "you are in for a real treat then."

Mary Jo and Jean just laughed and followed them into the bedroom.

FOUR

THE BEDROOM ONLY had a bed with a stained old mattress on it and a dresser that had one drawer missing. Tate Sones was tied to the frame of the room's small closet, sitting on the floor, his hands tied behind his back. A black zip-tie held his legs together at the ankles.

He had on an expensive silk suit, black dress shoes, and black dress socks. Mary Jo wagered Sones never thought that he and his expensive silk suit would end up on a dirty apartment floor.

All of them stood in silence and watched as Sones slowly came to.

At first he looked worried and confused.

Then he saw the four of them standing around in front of where he was tied and he looked scared.

Then he recognized Bonnie and got angry.

Red-in-the-face angry.

Confusion, fear, and then anger. The three phases of a hostage waking up. They all followed exactly the same pattern, some slower than others. Mary Jo had seen it more times than she wanted to think about.

Good old Tate Sones was one of the fast ones, going through all three phases in less than a minute.

He fought for a second at what tied him to the closet frame, then realized that was fruitless and squared his shoulders and glared at Bonnie.

"You think he seems a little angry?" Bonnie asked, smiling at Susan.

Mary Jo laughed. She was starting to like this young assassin more and more.

Susan just laughed as well as Mary Jo went over to the old dresser and picked up what looked to be a small dart. Then, as Sones struggled, she moved over and jabbed him through his fine silk suit into his shoulder.

"What did you just give me?" he demanded.

Mary Jo wasn't going to tell him it was an ancient and very powerful truth drug that made it impossible to not answer questions directly.

Mary Jo put the dart back on top of the dresser and returned to her spot near the foot of the bed beside Jean.

Jean took out a pad of paper from her back pants pocket and a pen and opened it. "I'm ready."

"Ready for what?" Sones demanded.

Mary Jo counted to ten, then with a smile at Jean, she turned to Sones.

"Did you hire someone to kill this woman?"

For a second Sones struggled as the drug took complete hold. Then he said flatly, "Yes."

"Why?"

"She had an affair with Holly Sones."

"You think that is worth killing over?" Mary Jo asked.

Sones again said simply, "Yes."

The drug had taken the fight and the anger out of him. Inside she knew he was screaming, but outside he was calm and without emotion.

She had to be very careful with her questions to make sure she got the answers they needed.

"Have you had other women or men killed that Holly Sones had an affair with?"

"Yes."

"How many?"

"Six."

Bonnie sucked in her breath, but said nothing. She clearly knew that only one person could ask the questions with this drug.

"Have you had others killed besides those who slept with your wife?"

"Yes."

"How many?"

"One."

"Who was that?" Mary Jo asked.

"A former business partner, Adam Hoss."

"So you have had killed seven people. Correct?"

"Yes."

"Do you have hidden bank accounts?"

"Yes."

Mary Jo glanced at Jean who nodded.

"Please give each bank name and country and account name and number and password associated with that account."

They all stood and listened and Jean wrote as quickly as she could as he calmly listed account after account, mostly in off-shore banks.

Finally he stopped, sitting calmly on the floor, staring straight ahead.

"Do you have a mistress?" Mary Jo asked.

"No," he said.

That surprised Mary Jo for a moment until she finally realized the next question. "Do you have a boyfriend?"

"Yes."

"Do you have more than one?"

"Yes."

"How many?"

"Three."

Bonnie just shook her head.

Mary Jo was feeling the same disgust. The man thought nothing of killing his wife's lovers, but kept three himself.

"Do you own your boyfriends' apartments?"

"The company does."

"Please give us the addresses and your boyfriends' names."

Sones listed three names and addresses and Jean wrote them down, shaking her head the entire time.

"Do you think you are hypocritical," Mary Jo asked, "killing Holly Sones' lovers, but having lovers of your own?"

"No."

Mary Jo had seen this for centuries, but seeing it again here, in this modern city, just disgusted her. She had been a man's property a thousand times over the centuries. The man had usually ended up dead fairly quickly.

Mary Jo knew the drug would start wearing off at any moment, so she indicated they should all go back out into the kitchen and they silently did.

"Wow, that's a piece of trash that needs to be taken out," Susan said.

"Yeah," Bonnie said, "and I'm afraid if we let him go what he might do to his wife after all this."

"No one said anything about letting that excuse for a human go," Jean said as she sat down at the table and opened up her laptop.

Mary Jo nodded. "Bonnie, do you have an offshore account we can land some money in? You can move it later."

"Sure," Bonnie said.

Susan knew the drill and helped Bonnie give Jean the account number and then Susan gave Jean her account number.

"Wow, this guy is loaded," Jean said after a moment. "I'm going to leave him a few thousand in each account. Make it look like he might be returning to the account."

Mary Jo nodded and watched Jean work. Mary Jo was so in love with Jean that sometimes she couldn't believe it. She could just sit and watch her for hours and enjoy every second.

Jean's fingers moved quickly over the keys. Mary Jo had no doubt that any of the other three of them could do what Jean was doing, but it would take them a lot longer. Jean was stunningly good at computers and financial accounts.

After just fifteen minutes, Jean smiled and said, "All of us are about forty million

Now Available
from all your favorite booksellers
in trade paper and electronic editions.

richer and the scum in there is a lot poorer. I made sure none of the money could be traced to us, but after a day move it again and spread it out."

"I think I really like working with you all," Bonnie said, smiling. "So what do we do with the scum in there?"

Jean looked up at Mary Jo and smiled. "How about we do a wicked witch on him?"

"Drop a house on his head?" Bonnie asked.

Mary Jo, Jean, and Susan all laughed and Susan hugged Bonnie around the shoulders.

"No, we're thinking of melting him," Susan said.

Bonnie laughed. "Oh, I like that a lot. And I can learn another trick. Perfect."

FIVE

MELTING TATE SONES was actually very easy.

Susan and Bonnie went and found a large metal garbage can and got it up into the apartment without being seen. The thing smelled of old wine bottles and some distantly remembered Chinese food.

At the same time, Jean went back to her and Mary Jo's place to get the bottle of acid.

Mary Jo, in the meantime, sent emails from a hidden account that looked like a government account to the three boyfriends of Sones telling them that they needed to get out quick, take everything that wasn't nailed down, and vanish. Sones and his companies were under Federal investigation.

Then Mary Jo made sure that Sones' will left his wife Holly all his assets, including all the companies, all his stock and cash in his regular accounts, and the penthouse apartment that they lived in. She was going to be very rich even without her husband.

Tate Sones was going to vanish without a trace and that will and personal instructions left her everything and in charge of it all. It might take a month before he would be declared officially missing and would take a year or more before the investigation would end and she could declare him dead, but Mary Jo had a hunch no tears were going to be spilled by Holly Sones on any of this.

In fact, all of the research they had found about Tate Sones over the last months showed that he had no real friends.

He would not be missed.

So when Bonnie and Susan got back with the garbage can, laughing at something as they carried it, they took it into the bedroom. Mary Jo followed.

Sones now looked panicked.

"I can pay," he said. "Anything you want."

"We already have all your overseas money," Bonnie said. "Holly is going to get the rest."

As Bonnie kept Sones focused on her, Mary Jo once again stabbed him in the shoulder with a dart.

He was out cold in less than a second.

Then she tossed the dart and the one she had used earlier into the bottom of the garbage can.

Then Bonnie and Susan hefted Sones into the can head first, making sure to tuck in his legs. They had to take off his expensive shoes and snap both legs to get him to fit.

Then all four of them used pitchers Jean had brought from their apartment to fill the can about a third full of water from the taps in the bathroom and kitchen. More than likely, at some point along the way, Tate Sones drowned.

Nobody cared enough to check.

Then Jean poured about half the bottle of acid into the garbage can, put the lid on the bottle, put the small bottle into her pocket, and stepped back as the acid combined with the water.

Mary Jo went over and opened up the window and then they all left the room, closing the door behind them.

It was going to smell like dry cleaning for about a day in that room.

But in a very short few minutes there would be nothing at all left of Tate Sones.

And the acid would vanish as well in about an hour, leaving nothing more than a three-inch layer of thick sludge in the bottom of the can that would harden like a rock in a few days.

Mary Jo glanced at Jean as they left the bedroom and headed for the door of the apartment. "A good morning. Anyone up for brunch since it's still a few hours before lunch?"

"I know a perfect place about five blocks away," Susan said.

"Hanson's," Bonnie said.

"Hanson's," Susan said, smiling at Bonnie.

"I'm buying," Bonnie said. "It's the least I could do for you guys not killing me this morning."

"Never would have happened," Mary Jo said. "But you can still buy."

At that, Susan and Bonnie went out into the hallway. They were totally focused on each other.

"Young love," Jean said, smiling at Mary Jo. "Isn't it wonderful?"

"It is," Mary Jo said, smiling at the woman she loved. "And after brunch, when we get back home, pour a couple of vodka orange juices and I'll show you some real young love."

"Oh, that sounds like fun," Jean said. "Can we skip brunch?"

Mary Jo laughed. "I think the kids need some company on their first date, don't you?"

"If they make it to the restaurant without spontaneously combusting," Jean said.

"I know that feeling," Mary Jo said.

"I'm feeling it right now just looking at you," Jean said, pretending to look very serious.

Mary Jo kissed her. Then, laughing, they followed the other two assassins down the stairs.

Mary Jo loved how this had all turned out.

A problem solved, money made, a clean death done, and the woman of her dreams beside her.

Just about as perfect a morning as any assassin could ask for.

PART TWO
A Puzzle

SIX

TWO WEEKS LATER, Mary Jo sat at her marble-top kitchen table, enjoying her morning routine, sipping her black coffee, and enjoying the morning sunrise over the city. Jean was still asleep and would be for another hour at least.

Outside, the sun was breaking through white spring clouds and yesterday's rain had done nothing more than make the city shine in the sunlight. Everything seemed to almost glisten.

She loved New York City more than any city in the world, and she had lived in most of them over time.

She felt lucky that Jean loved New York as much as she did. They would end up taking jobs that took them out of the city, but this would be their home. The place they would return to.

And to this penthouse, which was perfect for them.

The ultra modern kitchen in their penthouse seemed to shine as much as the city beyond the windows. They had white cabinets, white marble counter tops, and beautiful red and blue mosaic backsplash that added color.

All the appliances were stainless and shined and their mugs and dishes were all in blues and reds as well.

It should have felt a little cold, but actually, with the big windows looking out over the rooftop and the city beyond, to Mary Jo the kitchen felt like home and very warm.

This morning she was almost absent-mindedly going through her routine when she got a message from Tate Sones, or someone claiming to be Tate Sones, asking when she would complete her assignment.

All she did was stare at the message.

Mary Jo had not given Sones a second thought since they melted him like so much gum on a hot sidewalk. And Susan and Bonnie were a couple now and seemed to be enjoying every minute of their time together.

But there was the message, blinking at her.

It had the exact same code as the original hire message and seemed to be clearly written by the same person.

But Tate Sones was dead, she knew that for a fact.

And the papers had run articles about the search for him, about how he had cleaned out his accounts and then vanished.

The message basically asked when Bonnie Malak would die. The sender clearly thought the contract was still in effect.

So carefully, Mary Jo went back to her original research on Sones. And once again traced the hire, as any assassin could do. You had to know who you were working for almost better than who you were being hired to kill.

Sometimes a lot better.

Everything came up exactly as she had discovered it the first time. Tate Sones, the very dead two-inch layer of goo in an old garbage can, had hired her. She was sure of that.

Mary Jo took another sip of her black coffee and then went back and once again carefully read the message that had come through the official channel from Sones. It was short as all messages were coming through normal channels.

"Approximate time of completion of contract 26-BM?"

And then Sones' client number.

She must have missed something.

For the next hour, carefully, one detail at a time, she went back through all the research she had done on Tate Sones, his wife, his many companies, everything.

She knew a number of things for sure. They had killed Tate Sones. Of that there was no doubt.

They had that right.

The police were now investigating Holly in his disappearance, as was expected, but they had nothing to go on but what appeared from the outside to be a bad marriage and a lot of affairs on both sides.

But the press clearly wanted to pin it on her. That had to be a lot of pressure for her.

They had found his empty overseas accounts, or at least some of them. So now the official story was that Sones had had something go wrong and cleaned out some of his accounts and fled.

And Mary Jo double-checked to make sure that the original contract had been sent from Sones.

It had been.

But now that clearly hadn't been the case. It had been sent by someone wanting Mary Jo to think it was Sones.

But why?

Sones had clearly recognized Bonnie and had told them he had his wife's lovers killed.

Suddenly Mary Jo realized her mistake. She hadn't asked Sones if his wife knew he killed her lovers.

Mary Jo pushed back from the computer and said, "Damn it all to hell."

"That good, huh?" Jean said from behind her.

Mary Jo turned around to see the love of her life in her white bathrobe, her short hair standing up in all directions, her wonderful green eyes half closed to the bright light of the kitchen.

Damn she was cute in the mornings.

Mary Jo stood and kissed her, then went to get her a mug of coffee.

"You want to tell me about it?" Jean asked.

Mary Jo handed Jean the mug, which Jean took in both hands. Then Mary Jo kissed her and turned her back with her coffee toward their bedroom and bathroom.

"I'll start breakfast and tell you all about it then."

"Wonderful," Jean said in her sleepy voice.

Mary Jo went over and closed the computer. They would deal with that later.

Then, with a long look out over the glistening skyline of New York City, Mary Jo turned to start breakfast for herself and the woman of her dreams.

It was a good morning.

Living in a penthouse apartment in New York City with the woman of her dreams made every morning a good morning.

SEVEN

THE SMELL OF frying bacon, fresh toast, and sizzling eggs in butter filled the modern penthouse kitchen and made Mary Jo realize just how hungry she was. Usually she had a small roll or Danish while working in the morning while waiting for the larger breakfast with Jean.

This morning, because of that stupid message, she had completely forgotten.

And normally their breakfasts weren't this lavish or large, but Mary Jo had a hunch they were going to need a large breakfast today to help figure out this crazy message.

"You know the smell of this breakfast alone is fattening," Jean said, coming into the kitchen looking fresh and awake. "And impossible to resist even in the shower."

Jean was wearing her normal working clothes of jeans, a silk blouse, and running shoes and she looked wonderful as always, her green eyes seeming to pick up the brightness of the city coming through the windows.

Mary Jo pointed to the table and went back to finishing up cooking while Jean refilled her coffee mug and went and sat down.

Three minutes later they were both eating, not really talking, just enjoying the beautiful day outside the penthouse windows.

Finally, as Mary Jo finished the last of her eggs and bacon, Jean said, "So what happened this morning?"

"Had a client ask for a completion time frame on a contract," Mary Jo said.

Jean looked puzzled. "I didn't think you had any open contracts."

Mary Jo laughed. "I didn't either."

She opened the laptop computer to the question from Sones and turned it around for Jean to see.

"That's the contract on Bonnie," Jean said, shaking her head and looking up at Mary Jo.

"And Tate Sone's contact identification," Mary Jo said, nodding.

"How is that possible?" Jean asked. "I distinctly remembered we did a wicked witch to that slug."

"We did," Mary Jo said, nodding. "And I spent a good hour making sure that we had killed the actual Sones. We did as far as I can tell."

"So that means this contact didn't actually originate from Sones," Jean said. "But I don't see how we could have missed that."

"We didn't," Mary Jo said. "It came from Sones. But I have a theory that Sones did not initiate it."

"The wife," Jean said.

"I forgot to ask the scum if his wife knew about him killing her ex-lovers."

Jean nodded, clearly thinking.

"That kind of guy would tell her what he had done to try to stop her from doing it again. More than likely it was some sick game they played with their marriage."

Jean stared at the screen, then up at Mary Jo.

"I'm betting his wife was keeping track of this one and maybe even trying to frame him," Mary Jo said. "Get herself out of the marriage."

"And now that he's gone," Jean said, "she's being investigated for his disappearance and more than likely can't yet get to a lot of the money and property."

"Even though he's dead," Mary Jo said, nodding. "She still needs to take him down."

"Wow, what a couple they made," Jean said, shaking her head.

Mary Jo laughed. "We aren't ones to talk. We kill people for a living."

"But only for money," Jean said, laughing. "So got any ideas of what we can do?"

"We first need to make sure that the wife is behind this," Jean said. "And I think we need to get Susan and Bonnie out of town to safety until we need them."

Jean nodded. "Yeah, if this woman is desperate, she'll hire some amateur and no point in having Bonnie take any chances."

Mary Jo agreed completely.

"I'll call them," Jean said, picking up her breakfast plates and also Mary Jo's. Then I'll do the dishes before they get here."

Mary Jo swung her computer back around to face her. "I'm going to dig deep to see if I can figure out where he came in and she took over."

"And watch for piggybacks," Jean said. "It might not be the wife, but someone trying to settle something with Bonnie and wanting to blame it on Sones and his wife."

Mary Jo nodded. "We are going to need to get from Bonnie everything she was doing around the time she had the fling with Holly Sones."

"Looks like we have a contract after all," Jean said, smiling.

"Only without a client."

"Nothing is ever easy with us, is it?"

Mary Jo laughed. "Well, I can think of a couple things that come pretty easy."

Carrying her cell phone that she had just dialed Susan's number on, Jean came over and kissed Mary Jo. "Are you calling me easy?"

"If the shoe fits," Mary Jo said, laughing.

Jean put the phone to her ear, listened, and then laughed. Finally she said, "No, we are not in bed and no we are not having sex and no you two are not invited for sex."

Mary Jo just shook her head as Jean went on to invite them over for a serious talk.

"And no, not about sex," Jean said, laughing and hanging up.

"This is going to be fun," Mary Jo said.

"It always is," Jean said, heading to wash the dishes.

EIGHT

BONNIE AND SUSAN had been stunned by the message that the contract was still being questioned. And Susan got a little angry when she realized that Bonnie was back in danger, past the normal danger that their job brought them.

This kind of danger was stupid danger. If an amateur assassin made a run at Bonnie, there was no telling who might be hurt.

All four of them were sitting around the large kitchen table drinking coffee. Outside the huge windows the city looked like it was starting to warm up. The moisture from the night was gone.

Both Bonnie and Susan wanted to help with figuring this out. But Mary Jo and Jean both made it clear that to start, the best way Bonnie and Susan could help was get out of town silently and quickly.

Vanish completely, as if dead. Leave Bonnie's apartment a mess, as if she had planned to return in an hour or so.

"And," Jean said, "make sure you are not followed in any way and pick up new computers and phones along the way."

Both of them nodded. They were pros. They knew how to do all of that.

"You want the option to say the contract has been filled, don't you?" Bonnie asked.

Mary Jo nodded. "If need be. It might be the only safe way to clear this and find out who is behind it."

"I agree," Susan said, touching Bonnie's arm for comfort. "I'm going with you and we have both done this before. We just vanish."

"Damn," Bonnie said, "I was liking it here."

"We'll be back," Susan said. "And I got a hunch it won't be that long."

"Set up a guarded and secure spot and don't do any research on this from there," Mary Jo said. "Let that be up to us here. We want to take no chances of you two being followed in any way."

"And move regularly," Jean said.

Susan and Bonnie both nodded. They knew the drill. They all did. They all used it after some contracts were filled and they needed to drop out of sight and change identities.

Bonnie and Susan would just vanish without a trace from their apartment. They would leave everything in place, including a radio or television on.

They would change identities twice before leaving town and twice more at points along their travel.

Mary Jo had always found the vanishing an interesting part of this job, certainly a challenging one. Almost as much fun to plan than the killings.

Almost.

"We'll be working it here," Jean said. "As soon as we have a plan, we'll call."

Both Bonnie and Susan nodded agreement.

Then, for the next two hours, detail by detail, they went back over Bonnie's movements for six months ahead of meeting Holly Sones, the time of the affair, and everything since.

Mary Jo wasn't encouraged. The information just wasn't much.

Bonnie had lived a typical assassin's life during that year plus of time. She had only done one job in Chicago where she had been married to a guy so that she could get in close and kill his father.

Except for the fling with Holly, there had been nothing that struck Mary Jo as odd. And actually, that wasn't odd either.

Jean also got from Bonnie her daily routine, where she shopped, where she drank, where she ate, everything. Even who she knew in her favorite stores by name.

They didn't dare leave out a detail on this. There was just no telling where this threat was coming from.

And to be safe, they got the information of Bonnie's last five years of contracts as well, just in case something or someone was surfacing from a previous time.

Finally, the four of them headed out for a lunch before Bonnie and Susan headed home to get ready to vanish.

As they hugged outside the restaurant before splitting up, Bonnie looked at both Mary Jo and Jean. "Thank you."

"Assassins have to stick together in this dangerous world," Jean said, smiling.

With that, the two couples went their own directions.

By tonight, if someone was keeping track of Bonnie, it would look like she and Susan both had vanished from the face of the planet without a trace.

Assassins could do that. They were all masters at it.

But Mary Jo had never imagined that the skill would have to be used to avoid a contract from another assassin.

NINE

MARY JO WAITED twenty-four hours to reply to the message. In that twenty-four hours, she and Jean had searched everything they could search.

They found nothing new. So they both felt they had no choice. They had to try to lure whoever was behind this out in the open.

So after eating breakfast together, Mary Jo sent the reply.

"Contract filled. Payment expected as agreed."

They did not expect a reply quickly. Clients seldom did.

They had hacked into all of Holly Sones' existing bank accounts, at least the ones that were free for her to use that they could find. She didn't seem to have many and was very careful with them.

Mary Jo's second half of her fee was two million dollars. Holly Sones did not have that kind of easy money anywhere that Mary Jo and Jean could find. And they were experts at tracking hidden accounts.

So if it was Holly Sones that had continued the contract after her husband's death, Mary Jo would not get paid.

Clients sometimes felt they did not need to pay an assassin after the job was done. That was always a stupid and very deadly mistake.

Clients also wanted to check on the actual fulfillment of the contract, which

Mary Jo hoped would bring out who was behind this.

In the last twenty-four hours, Jean had set up cameras and listening devices in the hallway outside of Bonnie's apartment and also in a number of well-hidden places inside.

Over the last month, Susan had still kept her place, but they had mostly been staying at Bonnie's place. Susan cleaned out every sign she had been in Bonnie's place before they vanished, including wiping it for fingerprints.

The cameras and bugs were extremely small and not the kind that could be scanned for or traced. And if touched, they would simply melt into what looked like a tiny pool of mercury.

Mary Jo had set up a full computer with a second screen on the kitchen table that tracked and recorded all movement around Bonnie's building from the hidden cameras, as well as from some standard business and building cameras.

They had also hacked into the security system of Holly Sones' apartment building, including the camera just outside her door on the hallways there. They knew when she was in motion.

They had also hacked into her online computers in her apartment. She only had one that they could tell, but she used a wifi connector, so if she started up another, they would have it as well.

They also turned on the camera on her computer without turning on the computer light, so they did have a camera of sorts in her apartment. Her computer was at a desk that seemed to be against one wall so they could see the living room and part of the kitchen and the bedroom door.

Jean had set up another major computer and second screen on the kitchen table as well for this job. There was still

room to eat at the table, but now it looked like a war room, which Mary Jo sort of figured it was.

One person sitting at the table could see all the screens, which were divided down into many images from dozens and dozens of cameras.

Then they waited, taking turns at the kitchen table, taking turns cooking and shopping.

One thing that was a trait of all long-term assassins. They were very patient.

Mary Jo and Jean were both extremely patient.

They would wait and monitor everything until something changed.

They expected to be waiting for maybe weeks.

It only took five days.

Late in the evening on the fifth day after Mary Jo said the contract was fulfilled, a man wearing a Yankees baseball cap, a light jacket, jeans, and Nike running shoes appeared in Bonnie's hallway.

Mary Jo was watching the monitors and shouted for Jean to join her.

Jean had been in her office doing research on some of Bonnie's older contracts.

The man in Bonnie's hallway knocked twice on Bonnie's door just as Jean appeared behind Mary Jo to watch.

"Recognize him?" Mary Jo asked.

"No," Jean said.

The man seemed to be about thirty, with dark hair under his cap, and very light skin. He had wide-set eyes, a solid chin, and wore a small moustache.

He looked both ways, then took out a key and opened Bonnie's door.

"Wonder where he got that?" Jean asked, making a note on a pad.

Mary Jo was wondering the same thing.

Mary Jo and Jean watched him inspect the apartment, the clothes still left hanging in the closet, the rotted food on the counter. The dirty dishes in the sink, the television still on.

It was clear, as Susan and Bonnie had staged it, that no one had been there in five days at least.

"I'm on my way," Jean said, grabbing a light jacket and a hat and heading out the door.

Jean was going to track the man as he came out of Bonnie's apartment. She had in an ear-wig that Mary Jo could direct her through security cams.

The guy hung around a little too long for a professional, looking through the drawers and actually studying some of Bonnie's underwear before tossing it back in the drawer.

Finally, he seemed satisfied and went back to the door and out into the hallway.

"He's on the move," Mary Jo said.

"I'm in position," Jean said.

Luckily, Bonnie's apartment had only been a few blocks from their apartment.

The guy went to the elevator.

"He's coming down the elevator from the looks of it."

"Very cocky," Jean said.

When the guy moved onto the elevator, Mary Jo switched to the building security cam inside the elevator.

The guy didn't even pick his nose all the way to the ground floor.

On the front lobby security cam Mary Jo watched him head for the front door.

"Front door," Mary Jo said.

"He's turning right," Jean said a few moments later.

Mary Jo switched to the hacked security cams and watched him stroll up the sidewalk. He seemed to be in no hurry and in no fear at all. He never once looked around to see if anyone was following him.

A complete rookie.

Mary Jo could not see Jean on the security cameras, but she knew she was there, following the guy.

They followed him like that for seven blocks until he reached Holly Sones' building.

"This feels too easy," Jean said as the guy checked in with the doorman and then went inside the building.

Mary Jo was feeling the exact same thing as she switched to a lobby cam to watch the guy wait for an elevator. But there was no estimating the amount of stupidity humans could display when it came to hired murder.

Mary Jo had seen it all.

TEN

MARY JO WATCHED through the apartment building security cameras as the man went up the elevator to Holly Sones' apartment and knocked.

"He's at her apartment," Mary Jo said.

"Staying in position," Jean said.

Holly let the man in and luckily they stayed in the living room where Mary Jo could not only see them, but hear them through the computer.

Holly Sones was a looker, as Bonnie had said. Short, dark hair, clearly in shape, and from what they had seen of her over the last few days in her apartment, a natural, black-haired woman as well.

Right now she was dressed in slacks, flats, and a silk-looking blouse with a white bra under it. She had her short black hair gelled up and from what Mary Jo could tell didn't have any makeup on.

The woman was just a perfect beauty. Mary Jo could see why Bonnie had a fling with her. She looked like, in better times, she could be fun.

The guy handed a piece of paper to Holly Sones. "Sorry, she wasn't there and I didn't leave it as you said."

"Has she moved out?" Holly asked.

"If she did it was sudden," the man said. "Dishes in the sink that looked to be a week old or more, television running, food on the counter molded."

"Damn it, just damn it," Holly said.

Mary Jo was surprised. Holly seemed genuinely upset.

Holly moved over to her dining table just on the edge of the camera and tossed the note aside, then dug into her purse and took out what looked to be an envelope.

She handed it to the guy and he looked at what was inside and nodded. "Any other errands you need, just call."

"I will," she said. "Thanks, Phillip."

Mary Jo jotted down his name as the guy left and Holly Sones sat down hard on the couch and just closed her eyes.

Mary Jo couldn't tell what Holly was doing. She just sat there dead still.

Either she knew she was being watched and it was a hell of an act, or she was actually very sad that Bonnie was gone.

Or not surprised.

Just no way to tell. The woman was that good.

"The guy's name is Phillip," Mary Jo said to Jean. "He's on his way down the elevator now. Holly seems genuinely upset or disturbed in an odd way that Bonnie wasn't there. Phillip had a note for Bonnie from Holly."

"Well ain't that an interesting little wrinkle," Jean said. "I'll stay on him, see where he takes us."

Mary Jo sort of watched Holly while mostly paying attention to helping Jean stay hidden from Phillip.

It wasn't a difficult task. Phillip seemed unconcerned and didn't even once look around. He clearly was either a master professional, which Mary Jo doubted, or he had no inkling of what was happening.

After fourteen long blocks, Phillip reached an older apartment building off of Lexington and went in.

Mary Jo quickly did a search for any cameras anywhere in the building but as expected there were none. Too low-rent.

"I'm going to follow him in," Jean said when Mary Jo told her of the lack of cameras.

Mary Jo had a twinge of worry about Jean, but this was the kind of thing they did. And Jean could be as silent as a slight breeze and just about as invisible when she wanted to be.

Mary Jo got cameras aimed at all four sides of the building while she was waiting for Jean to check in.

"Apartment 1702," Jean whispered.

Mary Jo pulled up the records of that apartment. Rented to a Phillip Stanley. He was one month behind on his rent and didn't have an internet connection.

"No internet," Mary Jo said.

"Headed for the roof," Jean said.

Jean would get up there and set up a small piece of equipment that would allow them to tap into all the wifi in and around the building. More than likely if Phillip had a computer, he was using someone else's unprotected signal.

Within ten minutes Mary Jo had him. He was using the wifi from a deli across the street. Mary Jo hacked into his computer and got into his camera and email.

At the moment the camera was useless since the laptop was closed.

"Got him," Mary Jo said to Jean. "Come on home."

"On my way," Jean said.

Holly Sones had spent the entire time on the couch, her eyes closed.

When she finally moved, she walked like she had done far too much exercise in one day toward her bedroom.

Tomorrow, if Holly Sones left her apartment, they needed to get in there and see what that note said. And get better cameras in the place.

And check it to see if others were watching her that she might know about, thus the act.

And if it wasn't an act, Mary Jo had no idea what it was. Why had she heard the news about Bonnie and then just gone silent and still?

Not a bit of it made any sense.

At that moment Phillip decided to open his laptop.

He was naked.

And Mary Jo got a clean, straight on look at his penis before he sat down.

He was a handsome young man, of that there was no doubt. But his penis looked angry. That was the only term Mary Jo could think to describe it.

Red and angry.

And it was very large.

The first website Phillip went to was a porn site for gay men.

And that went on until Jean got back and just laughed.

Mary Jo was far from a prude and had done just about everything sexually in her centuries alive. But there were just some things not meant to be watched or seen.

Phillip making his large penis even redder and angrier was one of those things.

ELEVEN

MARY JO AND Jean traded off watching both Phillip and Holly Sones through the night, as well as checking all of Phillip's email and keeping an eye on Bonnie's apartment to see if anyone else came to check on her.

Nothing.

By sunrise, Mary Jo had a sinking feeling they were on the wrong track. And they had no leads at all.

Not a one.

As the sun came streaming into the kitchen showing that the day was going to be another wonderful spring day in the city, Mary Jo and Jean talked about what to do next.

They had one major area that was bothering them both.

Why did Sones take out the contract on Bonnie, if he actually did?

Two things could have happened there. First, somehow, the tracking back to

Sones had tricked them and was still tricking them and it was really someone else.

To Mary Jo that seemed almost impossible considering her and Jean's skills. But they were going to continue to check that, over and over.

Second, Sones really did take out the contract and someone had known about it and stepped in for him for some reason.

Those seemed to be the only two logical explanations for what was happening with that new message. And they had gotten no response yet on payment.

Enough time had passed, so both of them decided that if payment didn't come in this morning, Mary Jo would demand payment and force the issue.

But Mary Jo, for the first time in a very long time, felt helpless. At any other point, if she demanded payment and did not get it from a client, she knew the client and could take action if payment was not given.

But this time they were trying to figure out who exactly the client was.

So they decided to ramp up everything. They added four new monitors on the kitchen table, basically making it impossible to eat sitting at the table anymore.

They set up the three computers and six monitors in a ring around the edge of the large table so that one person could see them all at all times.

And they double-checked all their security measures just to make sure no one could piggyback on any of their signals or trace anything back to them in any way.

They both decided they would do that security check plus others every two hours, if not more often.

This morning, if Holly Sones stayed in her normal routine, she would be going for a spa treatment, the most ideal place

to pass on messages. So after breakfast, Jean had gone into the spa ahead of time and planted cameras and listening devices, pretending she was a health inspector. Those devices were now up on a multi-image screen as well.

And they had the spa computers and security system hacked.

They also had control of Philip's computer and any access to any server access he might make from the apartment. They had also cloned his phone so they knew where he was at all times as well.

So when Holly Sones went down to get into her limo to be taken to the spa, Jean was ready and within ten minutes she was in the Sones luxury penthouse apartment.

Mary Jo watched her as well as she set up cameras one-by-one and made sure they were connected. Mary Jo also watched Phillip and Holly Sones and Bonnie's apartment.

Jean had first scanned the Sones' apartment for any kind of devices and found none at all. And the Sones' phone wasn't even tapped which surprised Mary Jo. She would have figured with the husband missing, the police would have at least done that.

Jean found the note Holly Sones wanted to give to Bonnie on the table and read it aloud.

"Bonnie, my husband has vanished. Would love to see you."

"Well, that was no help either," Mary Jo said to Jean who just nodded.

Jean replaced the note exactly where she had found it and finished placing the cameras and listening devices.

In the spa, Holly met a woman by the name of Stephanie, who would take care of her through the two hours. Stephanie seemed to be one of those gym rats with false boobs, arms a little too strong, and a tiny waist. Her hair was cut short and was a dark brown with highlights.

Within ten minutes, by the time Jean was leaving the Sones' apartment, Mary Jo knew a lot about Stephanie. She was a divorced mother of a six-year-old daughter who was in a summer program.

She had no extra money in her accounts past a small savings account and seemed to be one of the many who worked from check-to-check to survive. She lived in a small place in Queens and groceries seemed to be her largest expense every month after rent.

There were no signs of large amounts of money hitting her account in the last year. Not a likely suspect, but at this point Mary Jo and Jean decided they would skip no one.

When you had no leads or even a decent clue, that's what you had to do.

And they had no clues.

Not a one.

PART THREE
A Surprise

TWELVE

MARY JO AGAIN sent the demand for payment on the contract.

Then they settled in to wait.

For two days they took turns at the computers, watching and listening to Holly Sones, Phillip, and Bonnie's apartment.

At times Mary Jo swore Bonnie's empty apartment was the most interesting viewing.

Holly Sones filled her days with nothing. She seemed to be busy, but when you actually thought about it, the woman did nothing. Most days she never left the apartment.

Phillip went out to a number of places, mostly just worked his job as a delivery boy for an Italian restaurant near his place, and watched porn for hours at night. How his penis withstood that kind of workout was beyond both Mary Jo and Jean.

During the waiting, Mary Jo and Jean kept checking back through all the history Bonnie had given them. Every detail they could find they double-checked.

No luck and no response on the payment demand.

Then everything changed.

Oh, wow, did it change.

Tate Sones, the guy they had melted, walked into Bonnie's building.

It took a moment for Mary Jo to even believe what she was seeing.

Not possible.

That flat wasn't possible, yet there he was.

Mary Jo shouted for Jean, even though Jean was in bed sleeping.

Within a few seconds Jean appeared at Mary Jo's side, pulling a bathrobe around her naked body.

Mary Jo pointed to the screen showing Tate Sones standing in the elevator on the way up to Bonnie's floor.

"Are you kidding me?" Jean asked.

Mary Jo shook her head and got some high-resolution images of the man to check for any mask lines. If it was a mask, it was one of the best Mary Jo had ever seen.

Jean patted Mary Jo and turned at a run for the bedroom to get dressed. She needed to be there to follow whoever this was when he left the building.

Mary Jo studied the guy. He wore a silk suit as the guy they had melted had been wearing. Same color, same type, everything.

He combed his hair the same way, was the same height and weight, and had the same size and shape hands.

They had melted this guy, yet here he was going to Bonnie's apartment.

"I'm on the way," Jean said from the front door and Mary Jo put on her headphone.

"You on?" Mary Jo asked.

"Got you clear," Jean said.

The guy didn't have a key, so he kneeled in front of the door and worked at the lock with a couple of picks.

Mary Jo quickly brought up what she had of the history of Tate Sones.

And then she went all the way back to his birth, his parents, everything.

He was not a twin. That much was clear.

There was no easy or logical explanation for what she was watching.

So Mary Jo sat and watched until Tate Sones got in the door.

He took out a handkerchief and covered his nose as he went in. Clearly the food Bonnie and Susan had left out now had a pretty good odor to it.

He went quickly into the kitchen, then into the bedroom, looking at the closet.

Then he looked around and nodded and went back into the hallway, not leaving any prints when he pulled the door closed.

"He's in and out," Mary Jo said to Jean.

"In position in ten seconds," Jean said. "But got a hunch it's not going to matter. There is a limo double-parked in front of the building."

Mary Jo got a camera on the limo and got the number from it. Then she quickly went to the internet services for limos in the city and hacked into the car, all before Sones got in.

She had three cameras in the car and his phone cloned and tapped before the driver closed the door and got around to the front.

"I got him," Mary Jo said.

"Grabbing a cab," Jean said. "And it's damn creepy. This guy even is the same height as the guy we witched."

"He's not a twin that I can find," Mary Jo said. "No evidence at all of a brother or even a half-brother."

"So who the hell is this guy?" Jean asked.

Mary Jo had no answer to that at all.

THIRTEEN

MARY JO DID some quick research as the limo worked its way through town. The limo was owned by Sones. The driver was a full-time employee of Sones' company named Steve. His only job was to stand ready at any time of the day or night to drive Sones where he wanted to go.

Mary Jo couldn't imagine a worse job, but the guy got paid a lot of money to do just that. And stock options.

The car and Steve the driver had been out of town for the last month, since Sones died. All records showed the car and driver had been in Chicago.

After a few blocks it became very clear where Sones was going. He was going home.

Mary Jo told Jean that and all Jean did was swear slightly.

Sones got out of the limo in front of the building carrying a briefcase and went past the doorman with a nod. The limo driver took the limo on around and into the building's parking garage.

"Think I should head in to be close in case this turns ugly?" Jean asked.

"No," Mary Jo said. "Nothing we can do if it does. Come on home and see if we can figure this mess out. I'll record the interaction between this new Tate Sones and Holly Sones for you to look at."

"On my way," Jean said.

Inside the apartment, Holly Sones was working at the large kitchen table on a crossword puzzle when Tate put his key in the lock and opened the door.

She stood and quickly moved to the kitchen for a knife.

"Anyone here?" Tate asked as he closed the front door and put his briefcase on a small table near the door.

Holly didn't take the knife, but instead went into the living room and into her husband's arms.

She actually looked relieved and happy to see him. That shocked Mary Jo more than she wanted to admit.

"Where have you been?" Holly asked after kissing Tate long and hard. "Everyone in this city thought you were dead."

"In Chicago in seclusion, working on a business deal." Sones said. "Sorry, I didn't know you were worried. Everything was supposed to be covered here for me. I'll find out what happened and make sure it doesn't happen again."

Holly nodded. "You are going to need to clear it up with the police. And seems a lot of money is missing as well. Or at least that's what the police said."

That caught Sones' attention. But he did nothing but shake his head.

Mary Jo sat back at that, thinking. Had they killed a Sones' imposter and this was the real guy?

Sure seemed that way now.

But why would an imposter have access to millions in overseas accounts? That made no sense. And know about Bonnie?

And be an identical twin?

The driver of the limo brought up Sones' two bags and then left.

Sones went back and got his briefcase. "I have something for you that goes along with the job I have been working on in Chicago."

He reached into his briefcase and pulled out a small pouch and handed it to Holly.

She looked in his eyes and Mary Jo could see the relief that the pig was still alive. There was just no accounting for taste.

Inside the pouch was a ring with the largest blue diamond Mary Jo had ever seen.

The damn thing had to be fake it was so large.

Holly gasped.

Tate took it from her and slipped it on her finger. "See, even fits."

She looked at it for a moment, then burst into tears and hugged him.

By the time Jean got back into the apartment, the married couple were tearing at each others' clothes and headed for the bedroom.

"What the hell?" Jean asked.

"See the monster rock on her finger?" Mary Jo said.

"Damn, is that for real? Amazing she can lift her arm with that on."

"Sones gave that to her and she evaporated like a drop of water on a hot sidewalk in August."

Jean looked at Mary Jo. "Think this is the real guy?"

Mary Jo slowly nodded. "He might be. I don't know, but if he is, then we melted a double he had set up to keep track of his wife and certain parts of his business and life. It never once occurred to me to ask the guy his real name when he was under the drugs."

"It didn't occur to any of us," Jean said. "So now we need to figure out what to do next."

"We need to figure out if this guy is yet another double and how the hell is Tate Sones finding and training someone to fix themselves so that they look exactly like him?"

"And more importantly," Jean said, "Why?"

Mary Jo only nodded to that question. If they found the answer to that question, they would have the answer to who the guy naked on the bed really was.

"His wife would have to be in on it," Jean said, watching them start into pretty aggressive sex. "Either that or she is as dumb as she looks."

Mary Jo honestly had no idea which way Holly Sones went on this. And not knowing bothered Mary Jo more than she wanted to admit.

"Wow, if she's not careful, she's going to cut him with that rock," Jean said as the two really got going.

Mary Jo just laughed. "At least then we would see if he bleeds."

FOURTEEN

JEAN WENT TO take a shower while Mary Jo started to dig even deeper into Sones' different companies. It seems his seeming disappearance hadn't affected them in the slightest.

In fact, everyone in charge in his companies knew he was fine. Only the press and the police had been in the dark.

And as she dug, Mary Jo found signs there were other businesses and companies attached to Sones' major conglomerate they hadn't spotted before. And she had a hunch there were a lot more overseas accounts than the ones they had cleared.

After the welcome-home sex was finished, Sones rolled over to take a nap while Holly took a shower, changed into her afternoon clothes, and went out to the kitchen to make herself a cup of coffee.

As the coffee was brewing, she dug into the back of one of the kitchen drawers and pulled out a jewelers' loupe and moved over to the sunshine coming in the window to really study the large rock on her finger.

The way she did it suddenly got Mary Jo very, very suspicious. This woman handled that loupe and inspection like a pro.

As she was finishing, her husband came out of the back with a towel around his waist. "Nice, isn't it?"

"Stunning," she said.

"Take a look at the rest of them," he said, moving to his briefcase and digging out another small bag.

She put a hand towel down on the table expecting what he was going to show her and he dumped what looked to be about twenty large-cut blue diamonds onto the cloth.

Mary Jo had no doubt that if they were real, the total in that bag would be more millions than she wanted to try to count.

Wow, just wow.

"They are stunning," Holly said, breathlessly, using the loupe to study one, then a second one while he poured himself a cup of coffee.

"Going to take us a while to move these through channels," Tate said.

"We're going to have to be careful with Sam vanishing the way he did," Holly said.

That sentence jerked Mary Jo back in her chair. They had melted a guy by the name of Sam, it seems.

Tate nodded. "I had a team a week ago tracking where he might have gone and what happened to the money in those accounts. They'll find him and shut him up."

"Unless someone already did," Holly said, smiling.

"Did he get a little frisky and you took care of him?" Sones asked, smiling at his wife.

She laughed. "He was fine, stayed in the guest room and never flashed me once. And besides, you know I wouldn't do that without you. What would be the fun?"

He laughed and reached in under the sink cabinet and touched a button and there was a click.

One of the upper kitchen cabinets moved outward and to the side and behind it was a wall safe.

Wow, that was something Mary Jo hadn't seen before. She got the keypad numbers as Sones opened it and his wife gathered up the diamonds, including her large blue ring, and put them all in the bag.

As the safe opened, Mary Jo could see stacks of money, numbers of other bags that looked like the diamond bags, and a stack of passports.

Holy shit did Mary Jo have this couple wrong.

Completely wrong.

These two were working together and were far more connected and more dangerous than Mary Jo had assumed.

This entire thing had just ramped up to a brand new level.

FIFTEEN

THAT EVENING, IN front of all the monitors, Mary Jo and Jean tried to figure out what to do next. It seemed logical that they should take out both Tate and Holly Sones. That would be the only way to make sure that Bonnie was safe.

If they were the ones who took out the contract in the first place, and Mary Jo and Jean could find no other person who might have.

And those two were not that careful, so it certainly wouldn't be a difficult task to complete.

"But if we do that are we going to know for certain that Bonnie is safe?" Jean asked.

Mary Jo had to agree that they would not, not until they found out for sure that Tate Sones, this Tate Sones, was the person who did the contract. And him going by Bonnie's apartment didn't prove it.

So it seemed like it might not be a bad idea to kick the hornets' nest a little to see what happened. And try to get some proof.

So the next morning, while Jean was doing the dishes from the breakfast Mary Jo had cooked, Mary Jo sent through the regular channels one more message.

"Contract is finished. Payment is now overdue."

The idea was that if they got the money, they would be able to trace it.

And if they didn't get the money, they would keep up the surveillance on Bonnie's apartment and on the Sones' pair and figure out what to do next.

Both Jean and Mary Jo tried to watch all of Sones' devices to see if the message even arrived in any of them, but it did not. That does not mean he didn't get it since more than likely he had far, far more devices in his control than they had found and accessed.

They waited two days and nothing happened. Not a response on the contract, nothing but routine for the Sones.

And no one showed up again at Bonnie's place.

At this point they might never know. And that was bothering Mary Jo a great deal.

But Mary Jo believed in their research, even though a Sones' double had fooled them the first time. Sones had done the contract.

But had it been Tate or his wife? Mary Jo flat wasn't sure which at the moment.

It was the third morning after the last demand.

Jean came out of the bedroom in her bathrobe, looking as wonderfully ruffled and cute as she always did in the morning. She had had only four hours sleep, since they were taking four hours on duty, four off on the computers.

Mary Jo was feeling the grind of the schedule, but over the centuries she had done far worse. But it would be nice to get this finished and back into a regular routine.

This morning, instead of a groggy look on her face, Jean had a smile and an actual twinkle in her eyes.

Mary Jo smiled back and laughed. "You wake up with a smile, that always means something evil is about to transpire."

Jean laughed. "You like that when I smile in the morning when we are both in bed."

"And as I said, evil is about to transpire. Very fun evil I might add."

Jean laughed. "My idea this morning is fun as well. Really fun."

Mary Jo checked the screens, then turned to face the smiling Jean.

"We need to figure out for sure if it was this Sones who took out the contract, correct?" Jean asked.

"We do," Mary Jo said, nodding.

"So let's take those diamonds and the contents of that safe off his hands," Jean said. "Then send him a message saying if he wants his property back, he must pay the rest of the contract."

Mary Jo just laughed. "That is wonderful, just wonderful."

And she knew instantly it would work.

Jean smiled and took her cup of coffee. "Thought you might like that one. Sometimes in bed I do more than just have sex and sleep."

"Yeah, but I like that sex part," Mary Jo said.

Jean just laughed and turned and headed for the shower as Mary Jo sat staring at the screens and chuckling.

SIXTEEN

IT TOOK TWO days for them to plan the theft of the diamonds. They could have really used Susan and Bonnie's help on this, but didn't dare bring them back just yet. Even as good as they were at staying hidden.

So Mary Jo had the duty at the computer screens, keeping track of everything to do with the two Sones.

Again Holly was headed for her two hours with her spa treatment in the afternoon. While Holly was gone, Tate would be in one of his office buildings in midtown.

Jean had no issue getting into the building without being seen, changing disguises twice on the way in just to make sure some stray camera didn't catch her. As Mary Jo watched and clicked off security cameras, Jean made it to the apartment.

Jean once again took out a device that scanned for any kinds of cameras or security devices. Besides the standard building ones in the hallway, she found none.

Mary Jo, sitting in their apartment at the computers was in complete control of the building security and actually opened the door for Jean.

Jean quickly went inside, checking for any unknown cameras or bugs and finding none there as well, even the most sophisticated ones like they were using.

She went to the kitchen and said softly to Mary Jo, "Okay, when I click this, monitor all alarm systems."

"I have it," Mary Jo said.

Jean touched the hidden button as Tate had done and the kitchen cabinet that looked like it was part of the kitchen and nothing more, clicked and slid out and sideways exposing the wall safe. Not even a dish inside the cabinet rattled.

"You are clear," Mary Jo said, making herself breathe.

Tate was still in his office and Holly was safely in her spa. No movement in the Sones' apartment building that seemed alarming at all. No silent alarms triggered anywhere.

Jean quickly keyed in the code to the safe that they had recorded Tate using and it opened.

"No alarms," Mary Jo said, again forcing herself to take a breath.

She would have been much better being the one in the apartment instead of behind the computers, but since Jean had already been in there once, they figured she was better to go back.

Jean quickly took out about five bags of what looked to be stones, then filled a backpack with stacks of hundred dollar bills and a notebook. Jean didn't look at any of them.

Then she closed the completely empty safe and pushed the button to have the cabinet retract back into place.

"Still clear," Mary Jo said to Jean who only nodded.

A moment later Jean was out of the apartment and headed down the back staircase as Mary Jo clicked off the security system recording for the staircase just before Jean got there and then turned it back on after she was past.

There would be no record anywhere of Jean ever having been close to that building, let alone in it, in any of her disguises.

Twenty minutes later Jean came walking into their apartment, smiling.

"Damn that was fun," she said. "Can't believe they didn't have alarms on that thing with that much money in there."

Mary Jo shrugged. "The rich often think that simply hiding something works. And for most crooks, the building alone would keep them out. I have to admit, never seen a wall safe like that one, though."

"It is pretty nifty," Jean said. "Let's see what kind of goodies we got for Christmas this year."

She dug into the pack and handed Mary Jo a heavy bag of stones.

It was the same one they had watched the Sones open when he had returned.

Jean went over to the counter and opened a drawer and got out a couple of jeweler's loupes and handed one to Mary Jo.

Mary Jo opened the bag and took out the ring first and then a loose stone. Both stones looked like massive blue diamonds. Both were over twenty carets and both had been cut perfectly.

"Wow," Jean said as she studied the stone she had in her hands.

Mary Jo was feeling the same way. These weren't anywhere near the size of the largest blue diamond in the world, the Hope Diamond at over 40 carets, but these had to be five to ten million each at least at a decent auction.

"Think they are conflict diamonds?" Jean asked.

Mary Jo shrugged. Conflict or blood diamonds were often mined in war zones to fund fighting. They were minded often using slave labor. Some treaties had cut down on buying and selling conflict diamonds, but this many beautiful blue diamonds together had to be something people didn't want others to know about.

Jean did a quick count and discovered there were twenty-two blue diamonds, all large, all real. Maybe three hundred million alone in that bag.

Mary Jo was stunned.

Jean took out another bag and opened it. About the same number of large pink diamonds, all perfectly cut and very rare.

The other three bags also were full of diamonds of various sizes and colors.

They put the five bags on the kitchen counter.

Mary Jo just stared at the five bags.

"Are we looking at a billion dollars in diamonds?" Jean asked.

All Mary Jo could do was nod. She had a hunch the number was that high. Not something Tate and Holly Sones were going to take lightly in losing.

As Mary Jo carefully checked all the monitors for movement anywhere, Jean piled the money from the safe on the kitchen counter.

"Looks like a couple million in cash," Jean said. "None are sequential bills, so no issue with them."

"Oh, good, we have some movie money," Mary Jo said.

"Won't last long with the prices of movies in this city," Jean said, laughing.

"Yeah, you have a point," Mary Jo said.

Then as Mary Jo kept an eye on the monitors, Jean took out the notebook. It was a bound leather notebook.

She opened the notebook and actually whistled.

She looked at a number of pages in it for a moment, then handed the notebook to Mary Jo.

It took Mary Jo a second to realize what she was seeing.

The book was full of overseas bank account numbers and passwords. Page after page after page of them.

"Oh, my," Mary Jo said, shaking her head and handing back the book to Jean. "I think we need to clean those out before he discovers the safe has been plundered, don't you?"

Jean looked at the book again, then at Mary Jo. "Who the hell is this guy? Really?"

"Someone who wants Bonnie dead," Mary Jo said. "For no reason."

"I still have Sones' bank accounts," Jean said. "I'm going to send Bonnie and Susan a message to be ready to start moving a lot of money over the next few hours."

"I'll guard the fort," Mary Jo said, indicating the computer monitors with all the video streams running. Then she pointed at the diamonds. "What the hell are we going to do with those?"

Jean shrugged. "We'll figure it out."

Jean picked up the diamond bags and went to the kitchen counter and opened up the one with the bowls, then put the bags of diamonds in a large porcelain popcorn bowl.

"For treats later, huh?" Mary Jo asked.

Jean just laughed. "Got to have something with our vodka orange juices, don't you think?"

Then with the notebook in her hand, Jean said, "I'm off to make us a whole bunch richer."

"Can we ever get too rich?" Mary Jo asked.

"Never," Jean said. "Top quality vodka is expensive." Then laughing, she vanished into her office.

Mary Jo turned back to the computers. Holly Sones was just finishing up her spa treatment, Phillip was delivering a meal, Tate Sones was still in his office on the 36th top floor of a building in midtown.

And Bonnie's apartment sat empty.

Mary Jo had a suspicion this was all just the calm before a very large storm.

PART FOUR
Let's Twist Again

SEVENTEEN

IT TOOK JEAN almost three hours to clean out over a billion dollars from hundreds of overseas hidden accounts and move the money to the four assassin's main overseas accounts.

All four of them were already rich beyond reason, but now they had become insanely rich.

Jean had called Susan and Bonnie and warned them to be ready, that they would have incoming money into their overseas accounts in very short order and to be moving it and spreading it around so that it couldn't ever be traced.

Mary Jo sat watching the monitors with her account open, watching Jean transfer in the money. Mary Jo would then move it into dozens of other accounts, let it sit for a few minutes, and then move parts of it again.

At two hours, as expected, Holly Sones returned to the apartment, but didn't open the safe. She went in to take a shower and then lay down to take a nap.

Tate Sones didn't make it back to the apartment until after five when they both changed and went back out again for dinner.

"So now what?" Jean asked. She was sitting at the computers and Mary Jo was just finishing cooking both of them steaks and a salad.

"I think we wait," Mary Jo said. "And do some research on those diamonds."

"Changed your mind on using the theft to trigger him?"

"We just took billions from him," Mary Jo said, smiling as she put both of the wonderful-smelling steaks on plates and the tossed salad in bowls. "He knows we won't give it back for two million."

"So we wait two more days and ding the contact person again," Jean said, nodding thanks as Mary Jo handed her the steak.

Mary Jo went to stand at the counter near Jean so they could talk and both eat and keep an eye on the monitors as well.

"My thinking," Mary Jo said. "If it's not them, we might get the real contract holder out of hiding. If it is them, it's not going to matter anyway."

Jean nodded. Then she pointed in the direction of the diamonds in the cabinet. "My sense is those things are a key to all of this."

Suddenly Mary Jo remembered a detail she had seen when researching one of Bonnie's old contracts. She moved her research computer from near the other screens and opened it quickly.

"I think you may be right," Mary Jo said, "but not in the way you are thinking."

Jean looked up from her steak. "Care to explain?"

Mary Jo held her finger up as a signal that Jean should give her a minute, then she found what she was looking for.

"About a year ago Bonnie had a contract to kill a businessman in Chicago. The guy had raped a young girl and was known for raping others. The dad of one of the girls took out the contract."

Jean said, "I saw that."

"The contract target was an internationally known diamond expert. Bonnie married the guy's only son to get close to her target and vanished three months after the funeral to move here."

"Well, ain't that interesting," Jean said, nodding as she checked the monitors and then went back to eating.

"The father who took out the contract stiffed Bonnie and then asked her to understand because of his family trauma."

"She didn't, did she?"

Mary Jo laughed. "Nope. But Bonnie got creative. They found the father strung upside down with a blue diamond hammered into his forehead. The police tried to pin it on the son, but nothing stuck."

"Shit," Jean said. "Think the son might be doing business with Sones? Damn, we got a lot of research to do yet."

"Eat your steak first," Mary Jo said, smiling at the woman she loved. "We'll

get to it. But now we know why the buyer of the contract isn't paying. If this is what I think it is, it's damn smart. They wanted Bonnie gone for revenge and Sones gone for business."

"Get two for a measly million," Jean said, nodding. "That's pretty damn smart if that's the play."

Mary Jo nodded. For the first time, all of this made sense.

And if it did work out to be true, a trip to Chicago was in their future.

EIGHTEEN

HOLLY AND TATE Sones came back from their dinner and ended up in their bedroom. Tate never checked his accounts and neither of them opened the safe.

Jean and Mary Jo had access to Tate's personal email account and when a notice came in that money had been removed from one of his overseas accounts, Jean had just scrubbed that email.

So until one of the Sones looked into the safe, they would have no idea that anything had happened.

Then, it was after Holly was in the shower and Tate was getting himself a snifter of brandy from their bar, that the crucial email came in.

It said simply, "Have you checked on our problem yet?"

Jean was sitting in the kitchen at the monitors. Mary Jo and Jean had both decided that Phillip no longer needed to be monitored. He wasn't a high enough player to have any part in any of this and both Mary Jo and Jean were tired of watching him do things to his penis that never should be done to any human body part.

So one set of screens and connects were gone, which helped considerably.

Mary Jo had been monitoring as many of Tate's email accounts as they could find. This one came through an account Mary Jo was sure Tate thought secure.

Mary Jo went to tell Jean just as Tate saw the message on a second phone. He shook his head and then replied,

"Apartment abandoned. My people say she vanished about two weeks ago. Do not contact me again on this matter."

Mary Jo had the email traced and they had been right. It came from Bonnie's pretend husband while she was doing the job, the son of the man she had been contracted to kill.

His name was Konrad and from what Mary Jo and Jean could tell, he had spent a vast amount of money trying to track Bonnie after she vanished. It seems the only way he found her was by accident two months ago. A friend of the family saw Bonnie in a deli.

Mary Jo smiled at Jean. Finally, it was all making sense.

"You want to have some fun?" Jean said, getting that sparkle of evil in her eye.

"Of course," Mary Jo said, laughing. "But can we do that and still watch the monitors?"

Jean laughed. "That kind of fun will be coming later, pun intended. I'm thinking we put a few breadcrumbs in the theft of all the money from Tate and point those breadcrumbs back to dear old Konrad."

Bonnie loved the idea. "I think we have the millions to spare to see what kind of fireworks happen, don't you? Switch and let me watch while you set that up."

Mary Jo took the chairs in front of the computer while Jean took her laptop back to her office.

In the next hour, Jean left a trail from one of Tate's emptied overseas accounts to Konrad, making it look like he had just been slightly sloppy with that one.

In the meantime, Mary Jo started into the extensive research it was going to take to learn everything about Konrad and the people around him.

Getting rid of Tate, Sones, Konrad, and others who knew about Bonnie was going to be the only way to clear this and make sure Bonnie was safe.

And that was going to take some work and planning. But at least now they knew for sure who had set up the contract.

And why.

NIINETEEN

IT WASN'T UNTIL the next evening, after Tate and Holly got home from dinner, that Tate opened up the safe.

Mary Jo happened to be on shift at the kitchen table monitoring station when he started and she called for Jean, who was in her office doing even more research on Konrad's family diamond business.

"Showtime!" Mary Jo shouted.

From what Jean had found, the diamonds didn't really completely belong to Sones, but instead belonged to a syndicate that brought in the large stones illegally and then worked them out through channels.

The system they used was why Sones had so many overseas accounts, most not connected in any way to each other.

Every time there was a new major sale, he opened a new account. Thus the ledger.

So Mary Jo and Jean knew that their theft was really going to hit Tate hard.

Jean arrived just as Sones keyed in the lock to the safe and swung it open.

"Here we go," Jean said. "I should have made popcorn."

"Popcorn bowl is full of a billion dollars in diamonds, remember?"

"Oh, yeah," Jean said, laughing.

Tate stood staring into the safe, then put his hand inside.

The safe was completely empty.

"Oh, that has got to hurt," Jean said, laughing.

Mary Jo laughed as well. Dear old Tate thought he was smarter than the entire world and was suddenly realizing he was not. Always painful.

Tate stood there for a few seconds, then staggered backward, calling for Holly.

He sat down at the kitchen table as Holly came in.

He simply pointed to the safe and she turned and saw the empty safe, then went to it and felt inside as Tate had done.

"Should have left something sticky and fuzzy in there," Jean said.

Mary Jo laughed at that image.

When Holly turned around, she looked like she was going to be sick. Her eyes wide, her skin a nasty blue-white that no live person should ever look like.

"Who did you let in here?" Tate asked her, his voice low and mean.

She shook her head, fear clouding her eyes.

"You job was to simply stay home and guard those diamonds and that money. And my book."

Suddenly he realized what he had said and sprung to his feet and went to his computer.

He clearly had the passwords and account numbers in another place because as Mary Jo and Jean watched and Holly Tate sat off to one side, Tate went through account after account, swearing softly each time.

Finally he got to the account they had left a clear breadcrumb to Konrad.

Three Mary Jo Assassin Short Stories
Available at your favorite booksellers.

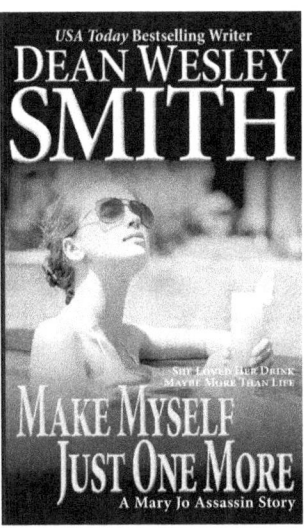

Tate clearly had some computer skills, enough to trace the trail and see where the money had landed.

Jean had taken the exact amount that had been in that account and put it in Konrad's account and made it look like it had been deposited at the same time as the original move.

"That bastard," Tate said, softly.

"Who did this?" Holly asked, her voice gaining a little more control. She came over and stood next to her husband. Clearly they worked as a team and for a moment that team had been strained.

"Konrad double-crossed us," Tate said. "He cleaned out all these surface accounts and took the diamonds."

"Why would he do that?" Holly said. "He's getting the same shares we are."

"That ex-wife killer of his has made him crazy," Tate said.

"But we did everything he wanted us to do with her," Holly said.

"I know," Tate said.

Mary Jo and Jean watched as Tate and Holly sat thinking. Finally Holly said, "Do you think Konrad is behind what happened to Sam?"

"Sam was the one in charge of taking care of Konrad's ex-wife," Tate said. "And I stopped by her apartment on the way in and seems like the job was done about the point Sam disappeared."

Holly nodded. "I had Phillip check on the apartment as well trying to figure out answers."

Tate nodded.

Suddenly Tate shook his head. "Son-of-a-bitch. That bastard isn't going to pay the professional assassin he hired to take out his ex-wife."

Holly looked at Tate with a puzzled look.

"If you don't pay those people, you end up dead," Tate said. "That's known when you hire them."

"I don't understand," Holly said.

"To cover his tracks, he used my account," Tate said. "Since I was already set up with the assassins."

Now Holly looked afraid. "Professional killers are coming after us, like the ones we had Sam hire for the others?"

Tate just sat there, nodding.

Holly looked like she was about to faint.

Mary Jo looked up at Jean and smiled. "He's pretty damn calm knowing he's going to die very shortly."

"And he doesn't seem that upset that he's lost a billion in diamonds and more than a billion in money," Jean said. "I'm smelling a very large dead rat here."

At that, Tate stood and went over to the sink and punched another button under the sink, one that he had to get down on his knees and reach around the garbage disposal to hit.

Another cabinet on the other side of the kitchen swung open and back, revealing yet another wall safe.

"We really need to start checking kitchen cabinet safes," Jean said, shaking her head.

Mary Jo quickly scratched down the numbers he hit to open the hidden safe.

Inside was more stacks of bills, more bags of diamonds, almost twenty bags, and another ledger book, this one gray.

From what Mary Jo and Jean could tell through the cameras when he opened it up, the ledger was full of more account numbers.

Mary Jo stood and let Jean sit down and Jean quickly tracked everything he was doing as he entered account number after account number.

Each of these accounts had more billions in it than the ones they had taken.

And there was a lot more accounts, including ones attached to South African businesses as well.

"Thank god he didn't get these," Holly said.

Tate nodded, focusing on the accounts and checking every one of them.

All Mary Jo could do was sit and watch, stunned, as the question kept repeating over and over, "Who exactly is this guy?"

TWENTY

WHEN TATE FINISHED with the accounts, he closed the book and put it back in the second safe. Then he and Holly both checked all the bags of diamonds.

Mary Jo figured there had to be billions of dollars in large diamonds of all colors. Far more than any market could bear.

Mary Jo had a hunch those diamonds and those overseas accounts didn't belong to any syndicate, but were Tate's and Holly's private fortune.

After they were finished, they put the stones back in the safe and then closed up both safes, leaving the one empty.

After a moment, their kitchen again looked like a normal high-end kitchen.

Holly went over and sat down at the kitchen table and Tate did the same, closing his laptop.

"So now what are we going to do?" Holly asked.

"First," Tate said, "I'm going to contact the assassin through channels, explain what happened, and pay the assassin twice the normal remaining fee."

"Oh, wow, we get more of his money," Jean said, laughing.

"Got to admit that's a pretty good idea," Mary Jo said, laughing with Jean.

"Think that will work?" Holly said.

"I don't know why it won't," Tate said.

"He's never met us, has he?" Jean asked, again making Mary Jo laugh.

"So what do we do about Konrad? And the rest of the syndicate?"

"We'll pay for the lost diamonds at fair syndicate value," Tate said. "After I hire the assassin who Konrad tried to double-cross and get free work out of them to take care of Konrad."

"We're getting even more money," Jean said, laughing.

"And again very clear thinking on his part," Mary Jo said.

"Wow," Jean said, "We stole billions from these two and they are going to weather it like a normal person weathers a late phone bill."

"Then," Tate said, "I'm going to get my best computer people on Konrad's accounts and take every damn penny he's got."

"Will that take down the syndicate?" Holly asked.

Tate shook his head. "No, I'll talk to Smith. We can find someone else to do what Konrad was doing."

Jean looked at Mary Jo. The look on Jean's face was very serious.

Mary Jo just nodded. "Don't worry, love, we'll make sure the syndicate goes down."

"Good," Jean said. "If those are blood diamonds, anyone selling them deserves what we can dish out."

"So we have a lot of work to do," Mary Jo said. "It seems I will be getting a new contract very soon."

Mary Jo pointed to the screen as Tate Sones typed in a message on his phone through official channels.

Less than ten seconds later, Mary Jo got the message.

"Double final payment will be sent in a moment to agreed-upon account. I was being framed by an associate not paying as agreed. I would like another contract. Triple your normal rates, half up front, half on completion of contract. Information of the subject of the contract to follow."

As they watched, Tate transferred four million from an offshore account that they had not stripped to Mary Jo's account.

She instantly moved it to more secure accounts.

Then she wrote Sones in return. "Payment received. Thank you. Another contract will be satisfactory on the terms you suggested."

Thirty seconds later Sones showed the message to Holly, who sighed loudly. Tate then sent Mary Jo the information about Konrad and his location.

"First time I've ever been able to watch a client do a contract," Jean said.

"Kind of gets your blood all a-tingling, doesn't it?" Mary Jo said, trying to keep a straight face.

Jean leaned in and kissed her. "No, but you get my blood tingling."

"When we get this job wrapped up," Mary Jo said, "More than your blood is going to be tingling, I promise."

"Oh, damn," Jean said. She kissed Mary Jo again and then said, "Lets hurry up and get this done."

TWENTY-ONE

MARY JO AND Jean decided that it was now safe to have Susan and Bonnie back helping, if the two stayed completely out of sight and stayed in this apartment.

So Jean called Susan and Bonnie and got them headed in.

"I told them extreme disguise," Jean said when she reported back to Mary Jo in front of the monitors.

"Going to be nice to have some extra help watching these places," Mary Jo said, pointing to the monitors.

Now, not only were there cameras on Holly and Tate's apartment, but also tapped into the security cameras in Tate's office and in Konrad's office in Chicago. Jean had a massive list of overseas accounts of both Konrad and Tate tagged to give an alarm if touched.

There were still alarms on Bonnie's old apartment in case anyone went in there, but Mary Jo and Jean were not monitoring it all the time any more.

Tate had decided to not contact members of the syndicate to tell them about the theft until he took care of Konrad. And both Tate and Holly were hoping to recover the diamonds from Konrad, as well as most of the money.

Mary Jo had gotten her three million dollar fee for the contract on Konrad and was deep into the research on him as well.

Both Jean and Mary Jo had decided since it was Bonnie's ex-husband that had taken out the contract on her, they would let Bonnie be part of the man's final moments, so he would know what a mistake he made coming after her.

Seemed fitting.

So Mary Jo spent the next two days researching every detail about Konrad and his relationship with the Sones and the syndicate. Jean dug into the syndicate.

She discovered there were five members. One in Great Britain that gathered the diamonds from many sources, Konrad and his jewelry import business, Tate and Holly in distribution, and one major diamond auctioneer who had very rich clients he dealt with behind the scenes for the top quality diamonds that came through out of the normal channels.

From what Jean could tell, all of them were very, very rich. And the five of them were responsible for a very, very large portion of the high-end diamonds coming into the United States.

By taking down the syndicate, they wouldn't stop the trafficking of conflict diamonds, but Mary Jo had a suspicion that they would put a very large dent in the top end of it.

When Susan and Bonnie arrived a little after six in the evening, looking like two men dressed in dark suits and white shirts with thin ties and carrying religious papers, both Mary Jo and Jean just couldn't stop laughing. Jean even asked if they had left their bicycles down on the sidewalk.

Jean promised them a good dinner and Susan and Bonnie climbed into the guest shower together to scrub off the makeup and hair dye and gel. After thirty minutes they came out wearing white, fluffy bathrobes, looking like themselves.

And clearly still very much in love, which pleased Mary Jo. She hadn't been worried, but sometimes a stressful situation like hiding and going underground might cause cracks in a relationship, especially a new one. For them it seemed to have strengthened it.

Mary Jo and Jean showed them the set-up on the kitchen table, then had them help her move the entire thing into the dining room table so there was more room for more people to sit and work.

That way, with the four of them back, there was room in the kitchen for people to eat as well.

They had the computers moved by the time Jean got dinner done, a wonderful pasta dish with soft, dripping garlic bread to die for. Jean could really cook. One of the thousands of things Mary Jo loved about her.

So all four of them took their meals into the dining room and sat along the edge of the dining table facing all the monitors and computers so everyone could eat and talk and yet monitor as well.

Tate and Holly Sones were home and getting ready to go out for dinner. They had not checked the second safe yet.

Konrad had left his office in Chicago and was in his penthouse condo there.

Nothing else was happening.

So as they ate, Jean and Mary Jo took turns explaining from the start how all the events had gone down.

When they got to Konrad, Bonnie just shook her head. "I should have killed that bastard when I had the chance. I had a hunch he was going to be trouble."

"It was only bad luck that he found you," Mary Jo said.

"And besides," Jean said, smiling, "It's made us all stupidly rich."

They talked for a minute or two about how shocked both Susan and Bonnie had been at the amount of money flowing into their accounts. It had taken them days to set up new overseas accounts and get money spread out and transferred.

"You ain't seen nothing yet," Jean said.

Mary Jo checked the monitors as Jean got up and went into the kitchen. A moment later she came back and handed Susan and Bonnie bags of diamonds. And gave both of them a jewelers loupe to look at the diamonds.

Both women were totally shocked.

"These are real," Susan said, her voice soft.

"I've never seen anything like them," Bonnie said, looking through another bag, then another.

"We are not sure yet," Jean said, "but we are afraid some of them might be blood diamonds. They most clearly have been smuggled in. The pink diamonds are not blood diamonds because they came from Brazil, but the ones from Africa we need to research more."

"That's why we are also going to shut down this diamond smuggling syndicate," Mary Jo said.

Both Susan and Bonnie looked up at her like she was nuts.

And at times Mary Jo thought that it was nuts to do this. There was no doubt this group of five in the syndicate had very powerful forces with them. But given enough time and planning, Mary Jo knew it would be possible to get the entire syndicate.

So for the next few hours, over cups of coffee, the four assassins talked and planned.

Mary Jo felt wonderful when Susan and Bonnie finally headed off to get some sleep.

Jean moved over and sat beside her in front of all the monitors.

"Feels good to have the four of us working on this, doesn't it?" Jean asked, leaning her head on Mary Jo's shoulder.

"It feels like we can do so much more," Mary Jo said. "And that is exactly what we need going up against something like this safely."

"Agreed," Jean said as the two of them sat there and watched as Tate and Holly Sones got home from a long dinner and got ready for bed.

Mary Jo knew that if the plan went right, it would be one of the last normal nights those two killers and jewel thieves ever had.

And that made Mary Jo smile as well.

TWENTY-TWO

Two mornings later, Mary Jo, Susan, and Bonnie were all headed to Chicago. The day was breaking clear and bright, which Mary Jo liked, since it was one of the first days in a week or more that she had been out of their apartment.

The air felt crisp and had that summer-morning bite to it.

All three of them were in basic disguises and all three were on different flights, different airlines, and would arrive at different airports.

They had reserved a large suite in a major downtown Chicago hotel and were planning on meeting there later, if they were not followed in any way.

Yesterday, Jean had discovered that both Konrad and Tate had enough security forces working for them to defeat a small nation's army.

And the security forces mostly stayed out of sight and in the background. In fact,

on the days that Jean went into the Sones' apartment, over ten people were watching the building in Tate Sones' employ.

Jean was so good, they didn't see her. And they were so good, she didn't notice them either.

Sones had one glaring weakness. He spent too much money on the physical security and not near enough on the expert computer security. That came from him thinking he was pretty good at it and those in his employ stroking his ego on that.

He wasn't going to live long enough to realize it was a new world for security.

Jean was going to stay back and watch all the monitors. And coordinate the three assassin's movements.

Mary Jo, for centuries had done all this alone. It felt wonderful to have two others with her and her partner in her ear clearing the path ahead for her. It didn't make her any less wary of problems or less alert, but it sure was a ton more fun.

Bonnie was already in the suite and unpacking when Mary Jo got there. The suite had two bedrooms, a large living room and kitchen area, and a bathroom that could fit perfectly in a mansion. Everything was in white and brown soft tones and the drapes were open showing the beautiful summer day over Chicago and Lake Michigan.

Mary Jo knew that Bonnie planned on going back to the exact same look she had when she was married to Konrad. Back then Bonnie had long brown hair and wore cotton blouses, a dress jacket, and jeans.

She really wanted to torture Konrad in his last few minutes of life.

Plus Bonnie seemed excited, yet cautious, exactly how Mary Jo was feeling.

Ten minutes later Susan arrived and kissed Bonnie and unpacked as well.

Mary Jo also unpacked and pocketed the large blue diamond ring that they were going to plant with Konrad. Tate Sones would recognize that when he got the death report.

The plan was to bring down everyone in the syndicate, but keeping the story that Konrad was the original problem seemed a safe thing to do in the meantime. And besides, what was one thirty-million dollar blue diamond when you had twenty-one in just one bag?

The assassins knew Konrad's security and schedule right down to the minute and the man clearly was a creature of habit, something that would get him killed very shortly.

In one hour, Konrad would go into a small, private gym for a quick workout after lunch, a quick sauna and massage, and then back to his office for the rest of the afternoon.

His security men stayed outside of the gym, waiting mostly near his limo. Mary Jo laughed at how a person confident in his safety never thought of the holes in his own life that let someone like her in.

The three assassins left the suite at different times making sure that Jean had the hotel security cameras off as they did. They had trashed all their luggage on different floors in garbage shoots. They would not be returning to the room.

Mary Jo's job was to go into the front door of the gym right after Konrad made it to the massage room. She was dressed as an executive in a large corporation would dress, with an expensive silk jacket and skirt, expensive shoes, a large wedding ring on one finger, and hair up perfectly. She also wore wide, round glasses.

In her large designer purse she had a very powerful, but not deadly gas that would knock out the eight people who were normally in the small private gym.

Jean would then make sure the gym's security cameras and system showed nothing as Susan and Bonnie came in the back and got Konrad.

A limo would be waiting around back and Konrad would get a quick antidote and then another drug to make him completely docile and able to walk, but not resist.

As Mary Jo went through the front door, the receptionist was on the phone. The woman, a young college-aged blonde with bright teeth and too much makeup smiled, finished up her phone call and then said, "Yes? Can I help you?"

"Building is clear," Jean said in Mary Jo's ear. "Eight inside counting two employees. I have the front doors now locked."

Mary Jo smiled back at the woman and said, "I would like to see about a membership. Let me get my wallet."

Mary Jo reached down and pulled a plastic gas mask from her purse and pushed it against her face.

Then she released the gas for the front area and stood. The young blonde's smile sort of froze on her face and she went forward into the desk, banging her head pretty hard.

"That's going to hurt," Jean said.

Jean could see everything Mary Jo could see through tiny cameras in the hairclip Mary Jo was wearing. A great thing was that Jean could also see behind Mary Jo.

Mary Jo couldn't even smell the gas because of the mask over her face. But she knew the people who were knocked out were going to taste lemons for a few days.

She went through the door into the gym, triggering gas as she went.

"Two in the men's locker room to the right," Jean said.

Mary Jo opened the door and let the locker room fill with the gas. She heard two bodies drop, but didn't bother to take a look. Those men would be out for about thirty minutes.

"Three women in the women's locker room on the left," Jean said.

Mary Jo did the same thing in the front area of the women's locker room.

Same thudding sounds of bodies dropping to the floor.

"All down except for Konrad and the guy giving him a massage," Jean said. "Heat signatures show the two men are through the second door on the left in a small room."

Mary Jo kept releasing the knock-out gas as she went, then opened the door, giving the small massage room a full dose as the door opened.

Both men were out almost instantly.

The only problem was that Konrad was on his back on the table and the massage guy had passed out with his mouth over Konrad's still enlarged penis.

Jean burst out laughing. Then she managed to say, "All clear, Bonnie and Susan."

"What's so funny?" Bonnie asked.

"Oh, you'll see," Jean said, still laughing.

All Mary Jo could do was stand there and shake her head.

TWENTY-THREE

MARY JO, SUSAN, and Bonnie managed to disconnect the massage therapist's face from Konrad's penis and get Konrad dressed before giving him the antidote for the gas and a shot to keep him moving but docile.

Susan had found his wallet and clothes and keys in the men's locker room.

As they were headed down the hall for the back door, Jean said, "Right on time. Twenty minutes before everyone starts waking up and wondering why they were sprayed with Lemon Pledge."

They got Konrad walked out to the limo and into the back seat while Jean made sure no security cameras anywhere caught the movement.

It took twenty minutes exactly to drive to Konrad's condo complex. They went into the garage and managed to get him into the elevator and to his penthouse without anyone seeing, thanks to Jean running interference and messing with some elevators along the way.

Konrad's penthouse condo was as Mary Jo would have expected. Filled with all sorts of expensive furniture, art, and other things that shouted money to anyone who came in. Konrad clearly was that kind of jerk.

In fact, the place shouted stupid money. The floors were bright white tile and the couches were white leather. Mary Jo pointed to one of them and said, "Who wants pure white on everything in a living room?"

Bonnie just laughed. "I had to use that stupid thing and these floors are always cold. Try eating buttery popcorn while watching a movie on a white-leather couch." She pointed to Konrad. "This idiot likes anything with a high price tag and his father was even worse."

As they dumped Konrad on his expensive white couch in his massive living room, Jean said, "All hell is breaking loose at the gym. I have the security cameras showing that no one is in Konrad's condo, but it won't be too long before someone heads to where you are to double-check."

Susan put plastic ties on Konrad's arms and legs and stepped back, leaving him sitting upright on the couch. He looked like he was sitting in the middle of a snowstorm.

Mary Jo quickly gave Konrad a shot in the arm to clear out the effects of the drug they had used to transport him.

Bonnie made sure of her looks and the position of her long-haired wig and stepped right over in front of him as he came to his senses.

Mary Jo was impressed. Konrad managed to maintain a sense of calm, but his eyes got mean and angry as he looked at Bonnie.

"Great seeing you again, husband, dear," Bonnie said, smiling.

"I thought you were dead," he said.

Wow, his voice was cold and nasty. Not only was this guy a superficial bastard, he was a mean one as well.

"Afraid the double-cross on Tate Sones just didn't work too well for you," Bonnie said. "Seems his wife thought I was hot."

Konrad started to come off of his couch, then realized he was tied up and stopped.

"Been great seeing you again, dear," Bonnie said, blowing him a kiss and stepping to the right to distract him as Mary Jo quickly came in from the left and stabbed him in the arm with the same truth drug they had used on the fake Tate Sones before melting him.

"What do you need from me?" Konrad demanded, still glaring at Bonnie.

Bonnie just smiled and said nothing. Now only Mary Jo could talk.

Both Susan and Bonnie stepped back out of the line of sight of Mary Jo since they knew she was wearing a camera and that Jean would be recording this.

"Please give us your full name," Mary Jo said, moving directly in front of Konrad.

Konrad hesitated, them Mary Jo could see the drug take over and Konrad's face went slack and he gave his full name.

"Confirmed," Jean said in Mary Jo's ear.

"Did you hire an assassin to kill your ex-wife?"

"Yes."

"Did you try to frame Tate Sones by not paying the final fee for the contract?"

"Yes," Konrad said.

"I think the Sones are going to love this home movie," Jean said, laughing in Mary Jo's ear.

"Do you have any hidden safes in this condo?" Mary Jo asked.

"Yes," Konrad said.

"Are there security alarms on the safes?" Mary Jo asked.

"Yes," Konrad said.

"Please tell me how to find each safe and the code to get into each one and how to shut down any alarm on each safe. One at a time please. Do not skip any detail."

Susan wrote every detail as Konrad told them how to get into each safe without setting off any security alarms. Mary Jo knew Jean was doing the same in New York and when time came to get into the safes, Jean would backstop them.

"Who else knows about your hidden safes and how to get in them?" Mary Jo asked.

"Carson Smith," Konrad said.

Mary Jo knew that Carson Smith was one of the syndicate members who was the contact in Great Britain for Konrad. They planned to take him out next.

"Do you have hidden overseas bank accounts?"

"Yes."

"Does the money from the diamonds go into those accounts?" Mary Jo asked.

"Yes."

"Are the account numbers and passwords written down anywhere?"

"Yes."

"Please tell me where."

"In the safe in the kitchen behind the cabinet in a gray leather book."

Mary Jo glanced at her watch. Her time with the drug was almost up.

"Are the diamonds you import blood diamonds?" Mary Jo asked.

"A few might be, but most are not," Konrad said.

"Are all of the diamonds you import brought illegally into this country?"

"Yes," Konrad said.

"Does anyone have any kind of record of the money or the diamonds you import?"

"No," Konrad said.

"List the names of those in your syndicate."

Konrad listed the five names they already knew.

Mary Jo could tell the drug was starting to wear off and Konrad was gaining on the fight to stay silent.

Mary Jo nodded to Susan and she came in from the side and stuck him in the arm with a needle.

Konrad slumped over instantly. He would be out cold for as long as it took for them to get him to his final breath. Then they would wake him up so he would enjoy his exit from this life. It would be the least they could do for an ex-husband of Bonnie's.

"How are we doing on security problems?" Mary Jo asked Jean.

"His security detail is still acting like chickens without heads at the gym," Jean said, "Not the brightest bunch, but they have their boss on the way, so I expect we have about ten minutes before they head your way."

"Let's go treasure hunting," Mary Jo said, smiling at Bonnie and Susan.

Both of them laughed and each headed for a different safe.

"Make sure we don't trigger any alarms," Mary Jo said to Jean.

"Got your backs," Jean said. "Make us rich. Wait, we are already rich."

Mary Jo and Susan and Bonnie all laughed.

Mary Jo punched a button near the top of a doorframe to have a wall panel slide back showing a safe.

If there were as many diamonds in these safes as Mary Jo thought there might be, this was going to be too much fun. She had always really loved diamonds.

And knowing that most of them were not blood diamonds now made this a little more fun.

TWENTY-FOUR

IT TOOK THREE of Konrad's carry-on shoulder bags from his closet to carry all the bags of diamonds and the five or six million in cash they found in the three safes. Mary Jo didn't even want to try to hazard a guess at the amount of money the diamonds represented.

Susan found the gray book with all the bank passwords and took a picture of each page and sent the images to Jean in New York.

"Wow, that's a lot of bank accounts," Jean said. "As soon as you three are in the clear, I'll start moving money."

"Any sign of any security activity in this building?" Mary Jo asked.

"None," Jean said. "But I wouldn't push it any farther."

"Cameras and area clear?" Mary Jo asked.

"All security cameras aimed in the direction of that building are off and I can see no one looking that way at the moment. It would be looking directly into the sun anyway."

Just in case, all three put on a white-haired wig and men's masks over their faces.

When ready, Susan nodded and she and Bonnie carried Konrad over to the patio door that led out onto a wide patio overlooking Lake Michigan.

"Really nice view," Susan said, as the moved him out into the warm afternoon air. A nice breeze was flowing off the lake, keeping the day from getting too hot, although the patio was clearly too hot to sit on for very long.

"One of the only things I loved about this place," Bonnie said. "I spent a lot of time out here to get away from this bastard."

Mary Jo cut the ties holding Konrad's legs and hands, then they stood him up and leaned him against the railing.

"Area still clear for take-off?" Mary Jo asked Jean.

"All clear," Jean said. "Give him wings."

Mary Jo stepped up and put the blue diamond ring in Konrad's front pocket of his pants, patting it so that it would stay.

Bonnie and Mary Jo held Konrad in place while Susan gave him another shot.

After a moment, he started to come around.

Both Mary Jo and Susan stepped back

The shot that Susan gave him would take about fifteen seconds to clear out the other drug completely and none of the drugs would be found in his system after thirty minutes.

"Thanks for all the money and pretty diamonds, dear husband," Bonnie said, moving up in front of him.

His drug-slowed mind clearly didn't completely grasp his situation.

Then Bonnie put one had firmly on his chest and shoved and lifted at the same time.

Bonnie was very strong and Mary Jo was surprised the young assassin knew that move.

Konrad, before he even realized what had happened, went over the rail backward, heading for the street below.

The penthouse was fifty-one stories in the air.

Konrad would be able to enjoy the view one final time all the way to the sidewalk.

"Damn that was fun," Bonnie said.

Susan hugged her as the three of them went back inside, took off their masks, and gathered up their luggage.

Ten minutes later the three of them walked out of the building through three exits, all cameras off courtesy of Jean in New York.

None of them looked like the three women who had come into the building.

All three had done quick changes in elevators on the way to different floors.

Mary Jo had started off the day looking like an executive business woman. Now she had long brown hair, a sweatshirt that said Packers on it, and jeans with tennis shoes. Her earlier outfit was in her large purse and she had the carry-on bag over her shoulder.

It took the three of them a full day to get back to New York. Bonnie and Susan bought a used SUV to drive and Mary Jo took the train.

Step one finished and finally Bonnie was safe from the contract.

Mary Jo messaged Sones that the contract was completed and that final payment was due.

Twenty-four hours later the money hit Mary Jo's account.

In the meantime, Jean had moved three-point-one billion into all four of their accounts from Konrad's overseas accounts. The four of them had spent most of a day creating new overseas accounts and moving money around to

give it some protection from any chance it could be traced.

Mary Jo always knew that she was very rich. Now she had no idea how much money she actually had and honestly no longer cared.

Living and doing her job was far more important than the money. It always had been.

The diamonds filled five large bowls in their cabinet. If they needed to make popcorn any time soon, they would be out of luck.

And now it was time to deal with the rest of the syndicate.

And then finally, at the very end, they would deal with the Sones. And maybe have a little fun along the way.

After all, what was life, and some death, without fun?

PART FIVE
Cleaning out the Riff Raff

TWENTY-FIVE

MARY JO, JEAN, Bonnie, and Susan spent five days researching Smith and his associates and his habits in Great Britain.

After the news reached Smith about Konrad, he made plans to fly to Chicago, which Mary Jo just found wonderfully funny. He was going to make it a lot easier to kill him than it would have been in England.

Mary Jo found that very considerate of him. Jean just laughed when Mary Jo said that.

Of course, Smith knew about Konrad's hidden safes and he was coming for the diamonds and all the money as soon as things settled after Konrad's "tragic accident" as the papers were calling it.

Konrad really had no family to speak of. His father was dead and his sister was pretty much in need of mental help most of the time.

And no one could seem to find a will, so that meant that Konrad's penthouse condo would just be locked up until things settled out.

When Smith boarded an airline for Chicago, Mary Jo headed for Chicago while Susan and Bonnie headed for Great Britain.

The plan was simple. Mary Jo would meet Smith in Konrad's condo when he came looking to open the hidden safes.

She would give him the same truth drug and get him to tell her where all his diamonds and money were. Jean would relay the message to Susan and Bonnie, who would gather up the spoils and head for home.

So once again, Mary Jo found herself in a white tile, white furniture condo overlooking Lake Michigan in Chicago.

Jean had the security cameras running on loops so no one in any of the security worlds would know she was there. And Jean also had the door locked and unable to be opened by anyone. She would let Smith in when he arrived.

Mary Jo spent the first hour there waiting exploring every detail of the apartment. Some of the art was original and expensive. And the wine in a controlled temperature room was superb. In some things, such as wine, art, diamonds, and Bonnie, Konrad had had pretty fine tastes. The pure white leather furniture on pure white cold tile was another matter.

"Smith has left his hotel," Jean said. "I'm betting his first stop is where you are."

"He carrying a large shoulder bag that looks empty?" Mary Jo asked as she sat down in a normal cloth chair in a second bedroom. Just about the only chair in the place that looked comfortable.

"He is," Jean said.

"Then no bet," Mary Jo said, laughing.

She was ready, the drugs she needed to use were on the kitchen counter.

"Susan and Bonnie landed in London yet?"

"Just did," Jean said.

"Fantastic," Mary Jo said.

She turned the chair so it looked out a large sliding door to another patio and the skyline of Chicago beyond. It really was a pretty city, a different city. She didn't love it as much as New York, but she still didn't mind being here.

"Smith is entering the building," Jean said a short time later.

Mary Jo put the chair back into the exact place where she had gotten it from and moved to the kitchen. She picked up one needle and moved over to a position behind where Smith would enter.

"He's alone," Jean said. "Opening the security lock for him."

A few long seconds later, Mary Jo heard a click as Smith unlocked the door and pushed it open.

She tapped the needle into his right arm before he even got a step inside and the fast-acting drug instantly sent him to the hard tile.

Mary Jo managed to catch his head before he cracked it on the tile. She didn't need him to give himself a concussion just yet.

Smith was tall, maybe six-two and very heavy-set. Heavy-set was a nice way

of putting it. The guy was obese. And he smelled of onions. Bad fried onions.

He wore an expensive suit and bright blue tie and had a really bad comb-over of dyed black hair. He also had a full forest of hair, more than on his head, growing out of his nose.

"Yuck. You would think he would pluck or shave his nose hair," Jean said.

Mary Jo just laughed. "Too busy trying to cover up his bald spot."

"Maybe he's growing his nose hair so they can replant it on his head," Jean said.

Mary Jo just laughed and moved Smith's legs out of the way and closed the door and heard another click.

"Security back on," Jean said. "Cameras still show no one entered the room, including Smith. I have Smith getting off five floors below and going into an empty condo there. Nifty piece of editing if I do say so myself."

"Thank you, my love," Mary Jo said.

Mary Jo took the used needle and moved back to the kitchen counter and put it beside the others. Then she took some zip ties and tied Smith's hands and legs. She had to pull them pretty tight because of all the flesh on the man.

Then, thankful that the tile was slick, she dragged him over to the white couch and left him on the floor, propped up with his back against the couch. No way was she going to try to lift him onto that couch. She could do it, but there was no point in smelling like bad onions the rest of the day.

Mary Jo gave him a shot to wake him up, then a shot of the truth drug, and asked him all the questions Bonnie and Susan would need to get his diamonds and money in London.

Then she added in one more question of her own. "Are the diamonds you smuggle into this country conflict diamonds, blood diamonds?"

"No," Smith said.

"How can you be so sure?"

"Governments are watching those diamonds too closely. We decided to take no chances. I do not buy conflict diamonds."

"That's wonderful to hear," Jean said. "But we're still going to kill him, aren't we?"

"Oh, hell yeah," Mary Jo said. "For no other reason in that he never cut his nose hair."

For the next ten minutes Jean just kept giggling.

TWENTY-SIX

THEY HAD DECIDED that it wouldn't be a good idea for a body to turn up in Konrad's penthouse condo, so Susan and Jean and Mary Jo had decided to do a sludge and flush.

Bonnie had no idea what that was and when they explained it to her, she just kept shaking her head and saying how lucky she was to get to work with three experienced assassins.

So after Mary Jo got all the information they needed from Smith, she stabbed him in the arm with a drug that sent him out cold again.

Then laying down a throw rug from a nearby bathroom next to the bulk of Smith, she tipped him over onto the rug and dragged him across the slick tile and into the main bathroom that had a large tub that streamed bubbles into the water.

She made sure his shoes left no drag marks on the tile. Then she tipped him up

into the tub and let him flop into the tub with a bang.

It took her a moment to first get the main drain closed, then get all his legs and arms inside the tub.

Then she turned the water on full hot, no cold, and went back into the kitchen to get the acid she would need.

She dumped the entire bottle in the tub when the water was about halfway up and tossed the bottle and the syringes into the tub with Smith. She turned on the air jets to start the bubbles in the tub and the water circulation, then went out and closed the door to the bathroom.

What would happen is that Smith would be basically dissolved by the acid by the time the water level reached the overflow drain.

The air bubbles and constant flow of new hot water into the tub would keep the entire mix moving and eventually, given a day or so, there would be nothing left in that bathtub but a nasty brown ring that could be explained away by Chicago water being left on for a long period of time.

Smith will have vanished into thin air, or actually, into the sewers of Chicago.

"Headed home, my love," Mary Jo said to Jean after she changed clothes and looks, put on a medium-length blonde wig, and made sure nothing was out of place in the condo.

"You are clear on security," Jean said.

"See you soon," Mary Jo said.

By the time Mary Jo caught the flight to New York and got back to their penthouse apartment, Bonnie and Susan were headed for Smith's flat in London. As with the other two members of the syndicate, Smith had kept all his diamonds in hidden safes as well.

And Smith, before his untimely accident in the bath, had been so kind as to give them exact instructions on all the security measures it would take to get into his flat, into the safes, and out again without being seen.

Mary Jo sat with Jean and watched as the two assassins quickly cleaned out the safes of as many bags of diamonds that Smith had had.

"These people had a lot of money in the pipeline," Jean said at one point, shaking her head.

Mary Jo had been thinking the same thing.

Susan sent Jean all of the passwords for Smith's many overseas and hidden accounts, then Bonnie and Susan went back to their hotel room to get some sleep and Jean and Mary Jo set to work making the four of them richer from all of Smith's accounts.

The next morning in London, Susan went out and bought some plain small mailing boxes, plain envelopes, and plain blank cards from about four postal offices. Then in four different postal facilities, she bought enough postage to mail each small box to another location in London.

Mary Jo and Jean were sound asleep still as later that morning in London, with gloves on, Susan and Bonnie went through the list of the two hundred top charities in Great Britain, packing two diamonds in each envelope and putting it in the small box, addressing the box, then saying simply on the card. "A donation from a grateful fan."

The four of them had decided that even though it was possible to get the diamonds back into the states, they had enough already and were going to get more from Sones. So instead of taking a chance on the smuggling, they would just leave the diamonds in London to good causes.

Besides, they were out of large bowls to put the diamonds in.

Mary Jo loved that idea more than anything. There was just no point in taking any unnecessary chances at this point.

Mary Jo was stunned at how much work it took for Susan and Bonnie to do this. One full day and into the night to get all the boxes ready and in shopping bags.

The next morning London time, in extreme disguises of thin men with gray hair and moustaches, Bonnie and Susan walked the boxes into numbers of mailing centers around the city.

That task alone took them most of the day as well.

And that night they were on a red-eye from London back to New York.

TWENTY-SEVEN

THE FIFTH MEMBER of the syndicate lived in New York as well and it only took three days to stage an accidental death and clean out his safes as well.

Now they had the diamonds in flour and sugar canisters on the counters that weren't being used as well as the large popcorn bowls.

Now, for Mary Jo, the real fun began. The Sones.

With the death of Konrad, the Sones hadn't seemed worried. They had talked with Smith a few times and he had promised them he had a good substitute and would get the diamonds back from Konrad.

So the Sones had stayed on their normal routines.

But then, when they couldn't get in contact with Smith after four days of him being in Chicago, they clearly got worried.

Tate increased the security, but all the increasing was physical security. Mary Jo thought that really funny. If those two idiots had a brain in their heads, they would be increasing modern security. Just stacking up more bodies around them would do no good.

Mary Jo was glad that the plan was to go slow, let the couple stew for a while, let them feel real stress, look over their shoulder for a time.

Jean had cameras on the Sones almost continually now and the four assassins took shifts watching twenty-four-seven.

After a week, a conversation between Tate and Holly finally changed things as they got ready to go out to dinner.

Mary Jo happened to have the shift and Jean was cooking, so when the conversation started, she called Jean in to watch as well.

"No Smith," Tate said as he finished putting on his jacket and straightened his tie. "I tried through five different contacts today without luck. He has vanished. So that means we're out of the diamond business."

"So any idea what we should do?" Holly asked, turning to have Tate zip up her dress.

Tate shook his head, but Mary Jo could tell Tate had a plan.

"Not a good idea," Tate said. "But I do have a few ideas."

"They are going to make a run for it," Jean said.

Then, as they watched, Holly nodded and went over to a chest of drawers and opened the top one.

She pulled out a pistol with what looked to be a pretty good sound suppresser on it.

"Wow, didn't see that coming," Jean said.

"Susan, Bonnie, get in here!" Mary Jo yelled to the back room. She couldn't believe what she was watching.

"What are you doing?" Tate asked, staring at his wife and the gun she held on him with a very steady hand.

"There is someone targeting the syndicate," Holly said. "As far as I can tell, you and I are the last people left standing. Actually you, since I am only along for the ride."

"That's why I think we should head out of the country," he said, taking a step toward her.

The gun in her hands didn't waver.

"I really don't think he should be getting closer," Jean said, laughing softly.

Mary Jo agreed. This was a side of Holly they hadn't seen before.

Susan and Bonnie arrived behind Mary Jo.

Bonnie said, "About damn time, Holly."

Mary Jo glanced at Bonnie. "You think Holly was capable of this?"

"Oh, yeah," Bonnie said, laughing. "That woman has some damn deep hidden pools in her."

Tate took another step toward Holly and she just shook her head. "You really are as stupid as you seem, aren't you? And take one more step and that stupidity is going to drain all over the floor."

Tate sort of jerked.

"You increased our security, right?" Holly said. "With more stupid guards. But did you ever think of increasing to state-of-the-art electronic security?"

"Our security in this apartment is solid," Tate said.

Holly just laughed. "You remember Konrad's little wife, the one Konrad hired an assassin to kill? Well, Bonnie is alive and she and her friends are listening to us right now."

"Not possible," Tate said.

Holly just shook her head. "You really are an idiot."

Mary Jo and Jean both sat back hard with that.

Mary Jo was stunned that their security had been seen through.

"Told you she was good," Bonnie said, laughing. "Never could buy her staying with that toad for anything but money."

"Or cover," Susan said.

Mary Jo was just shocked because Holly had not let on in the slightest that she knew she was being watched. Not even a slight slip. That took assassin training.

Mary Jo glanced back at Bonnie who was beaming.

"Did you know Holly was an assassin?"

The smile drained from Bonnie's face. "Not a chance. I would have known that."

Susan put her arm around Bonnie and hugged her. "I still love you."

"She's not," Bonnie said, shaking her head. "She can't be."

"If she knew we were watching her all this time and never once slipped," Jean said, "she's trained like we are."

"Shit," Bonnie said.

"So what do you want?" Tate asked Holly, his voice low and mean and clearly angry.

"I need you to vanish like Sam did," Holly said. "You have lived out your usefulness as a cover for me. I can get a few more years as your widow, so time to make that a reality."

Mary Jo was stunned as Holly, while holding the gun steady with her right hand, flicked a hidden dart at Tate with her left.

The dart went right through his suit coat on his shoulder.

He looked at it and then slumped to the ground.

"Yup, she's an assassin," Jean said. "No blood."

Holly put the gun back in her drawer, then looked directly into the camera they had planted near the top edge of the bedroom. A camera no one should be able to see.

"Bonnie?" Holly asked. "If you wouldn't mind, I could use a little help from you and your friends."

TWENTY-EIGHT

JEAN PUSHED BACK from the computer and went for her cell phone.

Mary Jo turned to Bonnie and Susan. "We need to confirm she is in the order."

Bonnie and Susan both nodded.

Jean came back and handed Bonnie her phone, then held up her phone. "I'm ready."

On the screens, Holly took the dart from Tate's chest and leveraged him up onto the bed and made it look like he was taking a nap. Mary Jo could tell the guy was still breathing. That was good.

Then Holly headed into her kitchen to get herself something to drink.

"Give her a call, ask her order name," Mary Jo told Bonnie.

Bonnie nodded and called Holly.

All four of them watched as Holly answered with a simple, "Yes."

"Your order name, please?" Bonnie said.

"Penarddun," Holly said.

Mary Jo knew that was a very old assassin name. Holly might very well have been with the order longer than Mary Jo. Penarddun was an ancient Welch legend name.

"Hold," Bonnie said. And clicked the phone on mute.

On the screen Holly sat down at her kitchen counter, sipping a glass of water as if nothing was happening.

Jean dialed the order contact number and after a moment gave her ancient order name.

Mary Jo watched as it was confirmed, then Mary Jo asked, "I need identification of an order member by the name of Penarddun."

Jean waited for a moment, then nodded and said, "Understood."

Then Mary Jo was surprised that Jean stayed on the phone, nodding. Then after a few moments she said simply, "Understood."

Jean looked at Mary Jo and she could tell that something was slightly off, but Jean didn't want to say anything. They would talk later.

Mary Jo loved how the two of them had complete trust.

She clicked off her phone and looked at Mary Jo and Bonnie and Susan.

"Holly is one of the oldest assassins the order ever put out."

"No wonder I didn't spot her," Bonnie said, shaking her head.

"So what are we going to do now?" Jean asked.

"My vote is we go help her," Bonnie said.

Mary Jo sat staring at Holly on the screen. "If that person really is Penarddun, which I have no doubt that she is. Why does she need our help?"

"Because of what she said to Tate right before she knocked him out," Susan said.

Mary Jo nodded. "Of course, he has hired a highly trained army to protect them."

"Do you think it's something that five assassins would have trouble dealing with?" Bonnie asked.

Mary Jo and Jean both laughed and Susan hugged her.

"One of us could do it with enough planning," Susan said. "But since Holly knows we are here watching, why not make it a lot easier and smoother."

Mary Jo glanced at Jean who just raised an eyebrow, but clearly agreed.

"Holly told us her plan," Mary Jo said. "She wanted to have the widow cover for a few years without worry. She might be able to stretch that into a decade of cover if she played it right."

"So good old sleeping Tate there needs to die cleanly, out in the open, and without suspicion on her," Jean said.

"And remember," Mary Jo said, "we complicated things by making his double vanish first, so the police are really paying attention."

"Makes sense she would need some help?" Bonnie said. She held up the phone that was still muted. "What do we tell her?"

Now Available
from all your favorite booksellers
in trade paper and electronic editions.

"Tell her," Mary Jo said, "to make sure Tate stays alive but asleep. Make him look like he's got the flu and is staying in bed. Then have dinner and then you and Susan will stop by with a plan after dinner."

Bonnie did exactly that and not a word more and hung up.

Holly nodded, glanced up directly at a camera in the kitchen and said, "Thank you."

Then she went back into the bedroom to get Tate staged.

And the four of them went to work on a plan to kill the guy, publically, and without anything pointing to Holly.

TWENTY-NINE

MARY JO AND Jean decided that it would be best for them to work the computers and security while Bonnie and Susan went in to talk with Holly.

So two hours later, as Holly was finishing dinner, Jean unlocked Holly's front door remotely and Bonnie and Susan went inside.

None of the army of men surrounding and guarding Tate and Holly saw the two assassins enter.

Mary Jo had told both of them they couldn't drop their guard. Jean had yet to tell her what she had been told by the order, but Mary Jo's little voice was shouting on this one.

Yes, Holly was an assassin, but a very old one, very set in her ways. She might know we are here and was planning to take us out. Who knew what rules she followed.

When Mary Jo said that thought aloud, it had sobered up both Bonnie and

Susan, especially with Jean nodding and agreeing with Mary Jo.

So Bonnie and Susan went in prepared for a fight with another assassin. They all hoped it wouldn't happen, but the two were ready just in case.

Holly didn't even get up from her kitchen table when the two entered and the door closed and locked behind them.

But when they came into the dining and kitchen area, she looked up from the table and smiled, then stood and moved to give Bonnie a hug.

Bonnie introduced Susan and Holly thanked them both for helping.

"We help each other when we can," Susan said.

Holly nodded. "I've heard that assassins were working together here in the city. In all my years, never heard of that happening before."

"We're having fun," Bonnie said.

"In more ways than one," Susan said, smiling.

Bonnie actually blushed a little, which Mary Jo found funny.

Holly laughed and said, "Yes, that can be wonderful fun."

"So we have some questions we need answered before we go any farther," Bonnie said.

Holly nodded and faced Bonnie squarely.

"We know who you are," Bonnie said, following the script the four of them had worked out. "Why do you want our help when you do not need it?"

Mary Jo actually leaned closer to the monitor to hear this answer clearly. To her it was the most important answer.

"I'm sure you know that the idiot husband of mine believed in physical protection instead of electronic as you use," Holly said. "And the army he hired is good for what it does. Alone, it would be impossible for me to get Tate's body out of this building with that kind of human blockade."

"You could kill him in his bed, from some slow-acting poison that no one would be able to trace," Bonnie said. "Have an ambulance take him to the hospital."

Mary Jo nodded. Again an important question.

"Yes, an obvious method," Holly said, "but I knew you were watching us and I knew it was your handiwork on Konrad and Smith to clear the contract from your name. Nice job, by the way."

Bonnie and Susan both nodded. "Thank you."

"So with knowing I had possible help," Holly said, "Tate's dying in the hospital from a bad disease seemed like a last option. I had a hunch that we could come up with better."

Susan and Bonnie both nodded.

Mary Jo just wasn't satisfied yet. All that sounded logical for a trap.

Then Holly smiled. "I had to live and have sex on demand with that frog for the last twelve years. Granted, I could have killed him at any moment and moved on, but he provided such a good cover to start and then the diamond trade got really interesting. I've lived for centuries and I didn't know I had such a passion for diamonds until I met him."

"Now we get the real story," Mary Jo said, sitting back.

Jean clicked off the mic so that Susan and Bonnie couldn't hear her.

"She's after all the diamonds we have in the kitchen," Jean said softly. "That is her real motive."

Mary Jo turned to Jean with a frown.

"The order warned me that lately Holly has gone rogue. That we should be careful."

"And?" Mary Jo said, looking at the woman she loved.

"We should take her out if we have the chance," Jean said.

Mary Jo nodded. "I suspected as much. We keep this to ourselves."

Jean nodded and clicked the mic back on.

"Bonnie, Susan, ask her if she has been ripping off the syndicate over the last ten years as well."

Bonnie said, "So, since the syndicate started, I assume you were also taking a cut as a sex fee that your husband and the others didn't know about."

Holly laughed. "Oh, heavens, yes. Tate and his fellow idiots had no inventory or even tracking system. They felt that would be too dangerous. And they had so much money, they couldn't even keep track of it. You got and cleared out one of Tate's ways of keeping track of almost a billion dollars and the book in the other safe has three times that much."

Holly pointed to the safe that wasn't empty. "You saw what was in that one and I have pulled back far more than that."

Mary Jo nodded. "She's for real."

"I agree," Jean said.

And Mary Jo breathed a deep sigh. This was going to be much, much harder than they had first thought.

THIRTY

THE NEXT MORNING, Jean was cooking eggs and bacon and waffles for the four of them. The kitchen smelled like heaven. Thick, rich, and mouthwatering.

The morning sun from a promised wonderful summer day in New York filled the kitchen with light and made Mary Jo feel much better after a restless night.

They had decided that Holly should just tell the guards that Tate was down with a flu and that she would be staying in with him.

Give them a few days to plan.

The four of them kept taking turns watching Holly. They had moved one computer with feeds to Holly's place into the kitchen just to make sure nothing went sideways.

And Mary Jo and Jean had told Bonnie and Susan, when they talked to Holly, to not talk about Mary Jo and Jean. If Holly asked, just say they had a little extra help.

Holly had heard there were assassins working together, but she only needed to know what two of them looked like at the moment.

Mary Jo still didn't feel right about what they were thinking, so in bed last night, with the two of them both listening, Jean called the order back to confirm what she had learned.

Holly was rogue, no longer following simple contract rules, and had killed another assassin. She should be removed if possible.

Mary Jo shuddered at those words, but understood. And now it made sense why Holly had known Bonnie was an assassin and yet had allowed a contract to be taken out on her.

No sane assassin ever went after another. That just wasn't done.

Until now.

So over breakfast, the plan was to come up with a plan.

At first they all ate pretty much in silence, with Jean glancing at the screen showing Holly in her apartment.

Mary Jo knew they needed to meet a few criteria on this. The plan had to have

Tate being taken out in public, in a way that didn't point any fingers at Holly.

The problem was that Tate was sedated and had, at Mary Jo's last count, at least thirty guards pretty much at any time in one form or another around where he was.

Jean had said the guy might have well been a majorette the way that group followed him down the streets like a parade. All he needed was a big stick and a whistle.

On top of that, Tate also ran a large consumer tech company that was completely legal and aboveboard as far as any of them could tell.

So killing this guy and not have any suspicion point to Holly was not going to be easy.

As they worked on the fantastic breakfast that Jean had fixed, Mary Jo finally broke the silence and said, "I think we just do a couple snipers on him."

Jean looked at Mary Jo and nodded. They had worked out the plan last night.

"What do you mean?" Bonnie asked.

Mary Jo shrugged and kept eating. "It is common knowledge he has a ton of security. So that tells the police he is worried for his safety. Right?"

All three of them around the table nodded.

"So we do two snipers," Mary Jo said. "One kills Tate, the other misses Holly as she is walking out of their building."

"That would certainly make that security force he's spending a fortune on look damned silly," Jean said, nodding.

"We would need to come up with some logical reasons why Tate and Holly were in danger," Susan said, "and plant the information so investigators could find it."

"We could have him carrying a bag of diamonds," Bonnie said. "And plant a bunch of connections with him and Konrad and his family diamond business in Chicago, including how maybe Tate had Konrad killed."

Mary Jo glanced at Jean, who was nodding.

"A diamond smuggling ring gone bad," Bonnie said. "All Holly would know as far as the police were concerned was that Tate spent a lot of time in Chicago. It was where he was when he vanished, so that plays in nicely."

Mary Jo nodded. She liked the idea a lot. The only difference was her shot wouldn't miss.

So over the next hour they hammered out a bunch of details, then before they started planting any kind of evidence, Susan and Bonnie went to talk with Holly.

Again, they got in and out past the army of security people without anyone noticing them at all. Jean working locks and cameras helped.

Holly liked the idea after she listened and asked a few questions and was willing to risk her life on their ability to hit a target from sniper range.

So that afternoon Jean and Mary Jo scouted out likely sniper's nests and found two with very clear and easy shots at Tate as he came out of his building.

And both had very easy escape routes, actually multiple escape routes.

So the plan was in motion.

And over the next two days, carefully, Jean and Mary Jo set the computer record of the problems with Konrad and Tate, making sure that once a police detective or computer forensics unit got on the trail, it would be followed.

Basically what they had was that Konrad had hired the hit on Tate from Europe before he was killed. The trail would show that a dead man had killed Tate.

Mary Jo loved the feeling of that.

And they also made sure that if someone dug deep enough, they would discover Holly was part of the diamond smuggling ring.

She was, of course. They just had to make sure the trail went through Tate to Holly in a few places.

And then they were ready.

PART SIX
Last Call

THIRTY-ONE

THE NEXT AFTERNOON, Holly got Tate dressed and then gave him a shot to bring him around and another to make him completely in her control. Both Jean and Mary Jo watched from their laptops in their sniper positions.

If anything went sideways, the entire operation would be called off.

Susan and Bonnie watched from their positions on a laptop as well.

Holly kept Tate's hair a mess and told the security detail she would be bringing him down to take him to the hospital and to have the limo waiting in front of the building.

The security forces did not argue with her.

Mary Jo had herself set up in an empty office four blocks from the front door of the condo complex and twenty stories up, with a clear shot. The killing field was the entire distance from the front door of the condo to the limo.

She had cut a simple hole in the glass at the right height for her rifle and had everything calculated and the rifle stable.

With luck, Tate's security people would be doing their job and keeping regular folks from walking through in front of Tate and Holly while they walked from the front door to the limo.

Jean was two buildings over and on the 19th floor, also in an empty office. Her shot was just as clear as Mary Jo's.

Susan and Bonnie were in the back of the condo, behind the building, waiting and watching.

Last night had been the dinner where Jean and Mary Jo told them what the real plan was.

Both of them found the information about Holly hard to believe, so on Jean's urging, Bonnie called the ancient order and asked about Holly. Susan listened in.

The order told Bonnie exactly the same thing they had told Jean twice, that Holly had gone rogue and if a situation came up, she should be taken out. She had become a danger to the order and to all assassins.

Mary Jo could tell the idea was hitting both of them hard. Very hard. It had hit her hard as well at first.

But by the end of dinner, the two were on board.

Mostly it was Jean who finally convinced them all the way when she said, "We were trained by the order, we owe it our allegiance since we have lived so many hundreds and hundreds of years looking young like this. We do not kill other assassins who are in good standing."

"That is why we did not kill you, Bonnie," Mary Jo said.

"But Holly has become a danger to the order and to us all," Jean said, "and I have no doubt she plans on taking us out for those diamonds." Jean waved a hand at the cabinet with all the bowls of diamonds in them.

"I have no doubt, either," Mary Jo said. "She has an unnatural hunger when it comes to those stones."

"So we have been given a contract by the order itself and we all need to carry it out," Jean said.

They had all agreed.

It didn't make Mary Jo feel any better about what they had to do, but at least they were not hiding information from Susan and Bonnie.

So when Tate and Holly went down on the sidewalk, Bonnie and Susan would get up to the condo and get the book and diamonds and money from the safe.

If they had time, they would use a floor and wall scanner to look for Holly's safe, but Mary Jo doubted they would have time. They were to disable every camera in the apartment as a last step on the way out.

Holly had Tate standing by the front door and she looked up at the camera in the living room. "I am on the move."

Mary Jo, over the centuries, had set up a lot of targets to get themselves into position to be killed, but never one quite like this before.

Holly took Tate and walked him zombie-like out to the elevator, contacting the security team as she did so.

Jean was tracking their movement.

A moment later Jean said to all of them, "Both targets in the lobby headed for the front door. Four guards have fallen in beside them."

Mary Jo could see that two guards were holding the front door open for Tate and Holly. The guards had moved the doorman back and out of the way. Very nice of the guards.

Mary Jo took a deep breath and focused on the scene through her scope. She had already done all wind and other calculations and was ready.

She went through her normal calming ritual and cleared her mind to only what needed to be done in front of her.

Holly and Tate came out the open front door, Holly on Tate's arm acting the part of a perfect wife.

They took two steps, exactly as Jean and Mary Jo had planned.

Mary Jo put a bullet center mass into Holly at the exact same time Jean put a bullet center mass into Tate.

The two went down, still together. The sound of the shot had not reached the bodies yet and everyone around Holly and Tate seemed stunned, frozen for that split second that often costs lives.

Mary Jo calmly took aim and put another bullet into Holly's head at the exact same moment Jean did the same for Tate.

"Targets down. Clear to go treasure hunting," Jean said to Bonnie and Susan.

Mary Jo calmly took apart her rifle, placing all the pieces in a trash bag, and making sure she hadn't missed a thing.

Then she moved over to a metal garbage can sitting against the back wall of the empty office next to a broom and dropped the gun into the can that was half full of water. She had filled it earlier.

A half a bottle of acid later, she walked out the door as the acid worked to dissolve the gun. The rifle had been specially made with no metal, so it would soon be gone.

Her gun would have not one bit of it left. Nothing but thick smudge in the bottom of the trashcan that would harden and no one would pay any attention to.

She knew that Jean would do the same in a nearby empty office where she had fired the shots.

All the security cameras in the buildings they were in had been jammed a half hour before Mary Jo and Jean came in and wouldn't be fixed for another hour.

Mary Jo went down five floors and changed her jacket and wig in the empty elevator.

By the time she walked out of the front door of the office building, sirens hadn't even started yet to get to the two dead bodies.

Exactly eleven minutes later, she was back in front of the screens in their apartment, watching as Bonnie and Susan did a quick search for Holly's hidden safe.

Then as Mary Jo watched, Bonnie smiled at Susan. "Holly said she had put up with Tate and all the sex for cover. Do you think she would have hidden all that in the bed's box springs? So she knew she was having sex on top of the diamonds?"

Susan laughed and the two quickly took the big mattress off the bed and did a quick scan of the box springs.

"There they are," Susan said. "No alarm, nothing."

At that moment Jean came in and kissed Mary Jo on the head and sat down to watch.

"They found Holly's stash in the bed," Mary Jo said.

Jean just laughed. "She really was out of date, wasn't she?"

"We're hiding a couple billion dollars of diamonds in popcorn bowls, so I don't think we should talk."

Jean laughed and kissed her and they went back to watching Susan and Bonnie.

Ten minutes later, carrying two large cases of diamonds and a backpack full of diamonds and money, Bonnie and Susan took out the last bug in the Sones' apartment and with Jean's help on security cams, made it out of the building just fine.

Twenty minutes later they were all together.

Jean picked up the phone and called the ancient order one more time to report that Holly had been removed from service as requested. She put the call on speaker phone so all four of them could hear the response, if there was one.

The person on the other end of the line said simply, "The four of you are commended. Thank you."

After Jean hung up, Bonnie asked, "How did they know there were four of us?"

Mary Jo and Jean laughed.

Susan hugged her. "How do you live for hundreds of years and still look so damn yummy?"

Bonnie just shook her head and said, "I have so much to learn."

THIRTY-TWO

IT TOOK THREE full days of moving money around to finally get all of Tate's money distributed and safe in overseas hidden accounts. Mary Jo had no idea what she would ever do with that much money. For now, it could just sit.

During those three days, Jean had also been busy planting little trails from Tate and Holly to Konrad and then to Smith. Jean told Mary Jo that she wanted to make sure that the police knew about the syndicate and how the Sones might have been trading in conflict diamonds, even though they weren't.

The police took the lead and the FBI got involved and Jean just sort of helped them form conclusions.

Bonnie had professional cleaners come into her apartment and take out all the furniture and everything and replace it with new and scrub down the entire place so it didn't smell.

And she and Susan went clothes shopping for her, since she had left so much of her stuff in her apartment and the smell had ruined everything.

In the meantime, she and Susan had been staying at Susan's place. And starting to work on a new contract that Susan had just been offered.

It seemed that life and death just went right on.

So finally, after it seemed everything had settled, Jean and Mary Jo invited Susan and Bonnie over to dinner.

They had one more thing to do.

On the big king-sized guest bed where Bonnie and Susan had spent the last weeks, Mary Jo and Jean had emptied all the big bowls full of sacks of diamonds on the bed, plus the cases and backpack full from the last day.

The sacks of diamonds in leather bags filled the surface of the entire bed.

"Wow," Susan said as they showed them the room.

"Needed your popcorn bowls back, huh?" Bonnie said, laughing.

"One hundred and thirty-one bags of large and rare diamonds," Jean said.

"Got any idea what we are going to do with them all?" Mary Jo asked.

She and Jean had talked about it last night and neither of them could come up with anything. Neither of them much cared for the diamonds, even though they found them pretty. Just too much of a problem to deal with. Assassins liked to keep their lives simple.

"Actually, we do," Susan said. "Let's go to a computer and if you would, bring up the news from Britain about the time we gave Smith's diamonds to charities."

"You thinking we should just give them all away?" Jean asked.

Mary Jo liked that idea, but to make sure the diamonds retained their value, they would have to do it slowly, over a long period of time. That many massive, rare diamonds hitting the market at once would kill the prices for decades.

"We are," Bonnie said. "Unless one of you wants them."

"Oh, god no," Mary Jo said and Jean just laughed.

The news from Great Britain clearly showed that the diamonds arriving at the charities had certainly helped each charity and caused a large stir. Turns out some major diamond brokers had to step in and help each charity with the safekeeping and appraisal and sale of the diamonds.

There was no clue as to the identities of the two men who were recorded shipping the packages full of diamonds.

So over dinner the four of them laid out a plan to deal with the diamonds over the next ten years. Each of them had decided to keep two bags of diamonds for possible bait for targets if something like that was needed.

The rest, Bonnie and Susan agreed they would handle, slowly, and in an untraceable manner. They said they had had fun doing it in Great Britain. They said it made them feel good.

Mary Jo just thought it looked like a massive amount of work. But they were willing to take it on between contracts for the next decade or so, and store the diamonds in a dozen safe deposit boxes in a dozen different banks.

"Big safe deposit boxes," Jean had said. "Really big."

So after dinner, Mary Jo got out a pitcher of fresh-squeezed orange juice and a bottle of the most expensive vodka she could find in New York, and made all four of them a tall vodka orange juice with a fresh slice of orange as a garnish.

"To being richer than Oprah," Susan said, offering a toast as they all sat around the kitchen table.

Mary Jo laughed and toasted and drank the wonderful-tasting reward.

"To being on the good side of the ancient order," Jean said.

Mary Jo toasted to that as well and took another drink.

"To not dying," Bonnie said.

All of them agreed and drank to that.

"To four great friends," Mary Jo said, offering a toast. "In a thousand years I never thought that would be possible."

And with that they all agreed and finished off their drinks and Mary Jo gladly made them all another.

Expensive vodka and fresh-squeezed orange juice. The drink of success.

—

Coming Next Issue in *Smith's Monthly*

#1...October 2013

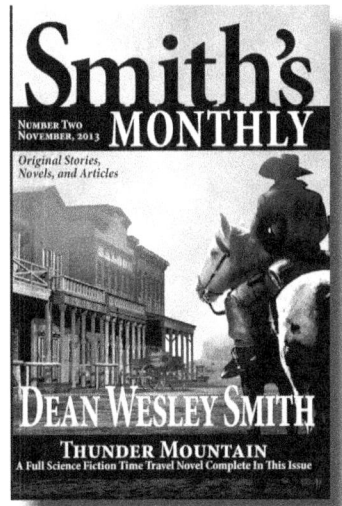

#2...November 2013

#3...December 2013

#4...January 2014

#5...February 2014

#6...March 2014

#7...April 2014

#8...May 2014

#9...June 2014

#10...July 2014

#11...August 2014

#12...September 2014

#13...October 2014

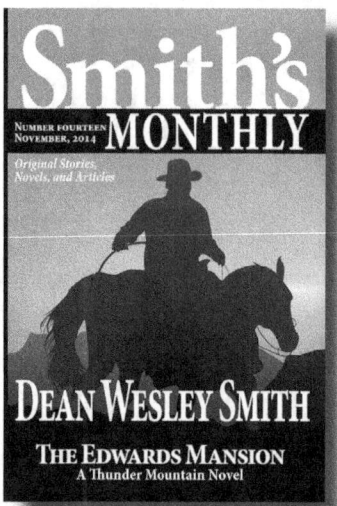

#14...November 2014

#15...December 2014

#16...January 2015

#17...February 2015

#18...March 2015

#19...April 2015

#20...May 2015

#21...June 2015

#22...July 2015

#23...August 2015

#24...September 2015

#25...October 2015

#26...November 2015

#27...December 2015

#28...January 2016

#29...February 2016

#30...March 2016

#31...April 2016

#32...May 2016

#33...June 2016

#34...July 2016

#35...August 2016

#36...September 2016

Thank You!!

I would like to thank the following wonderful people who support my blog and my work through Patreon. Your support is very important to me. Thanks!

Irette Y Patterson
Kathryn Rooney
Erick Lindman
Christopher Ridge
Raphael Husbands
James Gotaas
milady133
Danica Oakley
Kenny Norris
Kate MacLeod
Leah Cutter
Leigh Anderson
Robert J. McCarter
Jennette Heikes
Jamie Curierre
Albert Lemke
Marsha Kessler
Diane Darcy
Robin Brande
James Husum
Terry Mixon
Shantnu Tiwari
Chong Go
Maria Grace
Gnondpom
David Hendrickson
Fen

Sherman Cox
Miguel Angel Alonso Pulido
Marian Goldeen
Michelle Tatam
J.R. Murdock
Gunnar Gunderson
Jesse P Thurston
coraa
Martin Barkawitz
David Beers
Leslie Claire Walker
Nancy Hendrickson
F.I. Goldhaber
Michael J Lawrence
Barbara G. Tarn
Anthony St. Clair
Ann Tucker
Karl Gallagher
T. Thorn Coyle
Cristof Jones Harrison
Tasha Turner Lennhoff
Brenda Smith
Kari Wolfe
Mary Jo Rabe

And a very special thank you to Betsey Wilcox.